CAPTIVE

Black Wolf Gorge 3

Gale Stanley

MENAGE AMOUR

Siren Publishing, Inc.
www.SirenPublishing.com

A SIREN PUBLISHING BOOK
IMPRINT: Ménage Amour

CAPTIVE
Copyright © 2012 by Gale Stanley

ISBN: 978-1-62242-053-7

First Printing: November 2012

Cover design by Jinger Heaston
All cover art and logo copyright © 2012 by Siren Publishing, Inc.

Printed in the U.S.A.

PUBLISHER
Siren Publishing, Inc.
www.SirenPublishing.com

DEDICATION

For all those who love the beauty and majesty of the wolf.

CAPTIVE

Black Wolf Gorge 3

GALE STANLEY
Copyright © 2012

Chapter One

"Ladies, it's one minute to countdown." The way-too-cheery bandleader looked straight at Janis. "Grab your dates."

Where is my date?

Janis's cherry-pie red acrylic nails dug into her palms. She tried to look nonchalant while she scanned the hotel ballroom.

Dammit, Roy. Where the hell are you?

One minute he'd been standing by her side eating stuffed mushroom caps and mini-hotdogs, and the next, he had his cell phone to his ear, already walking away and mumbling something unintelligible.

Shit! Shit! Shit! Her first real New Year's date in eons, and she was destined to stand in the corner alone at midnight.

The floor-to-ceiling windows framed fireworks that lit up the sky, and over her head, multicolored balloons swarmed, waiting for their cue. But the magical night had all but lost its luster.

Janis felt like Cinderella at the ball. At the stroke of twelve, the spell would be broken, and instead of a prince by her side, she'd be alone like always. She should have known that having a man like Roy interested in her was too good to be true.

"Ten!"

A drink would help. She made her way to the bar and asked for one glass of champagne. The bartender gave her a pitying look as he handed over the flute. Did everyone here feel sorry for her? The last thing she wanted on New Year's Eve was a pity party. Screw them. At least she wasn't working.

"Nine!"

Janis took a sip and peered over the rim of her glass. She spotted Roy headed her way, and her eyes went heavenward.

Thank you, Lord!

She plastered a smile on her face and promised herself she wouldn't bawl him out.

"Eight!"

Roy blithely sidestepped other partygoers in his haste. Maybe he did have an important call. She really had to stop belittling herself.

"Seven!"

She downed the rest of her champagne and set the glass on the bar. Determined to be by Roy's side at midnight, she started walking toward him.

He really did look handsome in his black suit. The lab coat he usually wore over khakis and a button-down shirt didn't do him justice. And the air of confidence about him added to his allure. He looked like he was in his element, whereas she was definitely out of hers.

"Six!"

Suddenly, a hand reached out and clutched Roy's arm, stopping him in his tracks. His head swiveled to see who'd waylaid him. A stunning redhead with Mae West curves flashed a big smile, grabbed the back of Roy's head, and glued her mouth to his.

"Five!"

Janis clenched her teeth so hard she swore she heard the enamel crack. She wanted to pull the skanky bitch off her date and slap her silly.

"Four!"

She'd seen the woman once before. But she'd been wearing a white nurse's uniform instead of a strapless black cocktail dress that fit her like a second skin. She sat at a reception desk in front of Roy's office and acted like his guard dog.

"Three!"

Maybe Roy needed a guard dog. His status at Philadelphia Hospital had grown since some mysterious benefactor funded a new addition. With the building complete, Roy had been named head of the Foundation for Infertility and Reproductive Medicine. The FIRM turned out to be a major coup for the hospital. The sprawling complex that had once been a public charity hospital had gained new respect and became a major player in the world of research. Roy had high hopes of achieving a major breakthrough in the treatment of infertility.

"Two!"

She'd been so thrilled when Roy asked her to be his date. He'd chosen to share his success with her and show her off to his colleagues. Now it looked like she was being played as his second fiddle.

"Happy New Year!"

At the stroke of midnight, popping balloons sent streams of confetti pouring over the excited crowd. She lost sight of Roy and the redhead, and she bit back hot tears.

The crowd shifted, and Janis caught a glimpse of Roy. She watched the redhead pull a tissue from a tiny beaded purse and dab at his face. She wanted to claw the woman's eyes out.

The woman had given her a hard time the day she'd stopped at Roy's office. She'd made a big show of checking Roy's calendar and letting Janis know she wasn't on it. If Roy hadn't stepped out of his inner sanctum, Janis might not have gotten to see him at all.

He'd brushed off her questions about the redhead. He paid the woman to screen his visitors. She had only been doing her job.

Had Janis been stupid to believe him? Her inner critic said *yes.* The subversive voice berated her. *What did you expect?*

She'd known Roy was out of her league as soon as she met him. His dark good looks drew glances wherever they went, but more than that, Roy was husband material—a doctor. The nurses probably swarmed over him like bees to honey. No wonder he rarely asked her to meet him at the hospital.

She'd been a fool, running out to get her hair and nails done. Buying a new dress. Suddenly she felt dowdy and unattractive. She smoothed the taffeta over her hips. The full skirt couldn't compete with the redhead's short, slinky model.

She tried to look invisible. Not that anyone would notice her. They'd all paired off, lip-locked and groping each other in an erotic celebration of the New Year.

Why had Roy chosen her when he could have had his pick of so many others? They had so little in common. He'd always lived in the city while she'd grown up in the wilds of Pennsylvania. He had degrees up the wazoo while she stopped at a high school diploma.

Why did she feel so inadequate around him? She did a bang-up job managing her brothers' apartment building, and she'd already signed up for classes so she could become a licensed real estate agent.

She'd given him all the power in this relationship because she'd viewed him as perfect. Obviously, he was far from it. If she couldn't trust him, then maybe he wasn't the man for her. Right then and there, she made a New Year's resolution. From now on she would speak her mind and stand up for herself.

Janis took a step toward the door. She refused to stand alone like some lovelorn loser while her date kissed another woman across the room. If she had to spend her New Year's in the ladies room, so be it.

Suddenly, strong arms circled her waist and pulled her in. Roy's distinctive cologne, a citrus fragrance, flooded her nostrils. Sweet relief filled her. He hadn't deserted her completely. Suddenly her new resolve kicked in.

Get a backbone, girl!

She would not let him get away with this.

She twisted in his arms, and he planted a big sloppy kiss on her mouth before she could open it to bawl him out. *Ugh!*

His kisses never made her toes curl and especially not with the redhead's saliva still in his mouth. Janis swore she could taste her.

But he held her so tight she had no choice but to endure his enthusiastic smooch. She detected interest in another part of his anatomy. The hard ridge of his cock pressed against her, finding her core like a homing pigeon.

When he pulled back, she lost it. She put her hands on his shoulders and shoved. "Where were you?"

Roy's hurt expression almost looked genuine. He backed off and raised his hands in surrender. "Hey, calm down. I'm a doctor, remember? My work doesn't shut down for the holiday like yours. His brow wrinkled, and his face took on a sullen look that signaled his disapproval. "Research takes priority over a holiday party." His back rigid, he folded his arms over his chest.

"Really?" She hated herself for sounding like a nagging shrew, but she was determined to stand her ground. "What kind of research were you doing with your assistant?"

"Oh, so that's what this is about?"

She took a deep breath and folded her arms across her chest. *This better be good, Roy.*

"You shouldn't jump to conclusions, Janis."

"I saw you kiss her." God, she wished she had some Maalox to stop the acid eating away at her stomach lining.

"No," he said sternly. "You saw her kiss me."

"What's the difference?"

"It's not my fault if the woman is interested in more than just working with me. I haven't encouraged her at all, but she's relentless. Took me completely by surprise just now. You know you're the only woman I'm interested in."

"And how would I know that?"

"Because I'm telling you."

She wanted to believe him. She had met some very pushy women in the city. It was a dog-eat-dog world, and people went after what they wanted with no thought of anyone else.

And she'd really hoped their dates would develop into something more. She'd always thought that by thirty-two, she'd be married to the love of her life and raising two kids. She enjoyed her work, but she'd give it up in a heartbeat if she had a family of her own.

He cupped her jaw and lifted her head so her eyes met his. "Believe me, Janis. That woman means nothing to me."

He seemed so sincere, and suddenly, she felt like a fool.

"Oh, well…Of course I believe you," she stammered and turned red. "I'm sorry." How did he always manage to turn things around so she ended up looking like the bad guy and apologizing?

"Well, no harm done." Roy grabbed her arms and pulled her in close. "Happy New Year. Better late than never." He stuck his tongue down her throat and ground his obvious arousal against her hips.

Janis threw her arms around him and tried to put some emotion into her kiss, but she couldn't get the other woman out of her mind.

Roy pulled back and smiled at her. "Now that's more like it. Let's get out of here. Have our own celebration."

Not quite ready to forgive and forget, Janis hesitated. "I thought we'd have a glass of champagne to toast the New Year."

"Sure. Whatever you want." He guided her back to the bar and asked for two glasses.

"To the future." Roy held out his glass.

Her hopes soared. It was the closest he'd ever come to talking about a future for them. She smiled and clinked his glass with hers.

They sipped in silence for a few seconds.

"I hope I didn't ruin your mood," Roy said. "The night is still young." He grinned at her.

She knew what that meant. Although she'd forgiven him, the idea of fucking Roy right now didn't excite her even the least little bit. That troubled her more than the redhead.

She'd drunk enough champagne to silence her inner voice, and Roy looked amazing tonight. Shouldn't the anticipation of sex get her a little hot? It wasn't like they were an old married couple. Even the married couples she knew acted like they were ready to jump each other's bones at a moment's notice.

Her brothers had the most unconventional relationship imaginable. They were both married to the same woman. Well, Jude had the piece of paper that made it legal. But his twin, Jonas, was just as much husband to Sable as Jude was.

They'd each fathered one of her twin boys. Evidently she'd released two eggs in her cycle and then had intercourse with both men. Each man had fertilized one of her eggs resulting in fraternal twins with two different fathers.

She hadn't understood at first, and when she asked Roy about it, his eyes lit up like a kid on Christmas morning. She'd never seen him so excited. He'd explained how rare it was in humans and that it happened more often in the animal world.

She regretted telling him anything because he kept bugging her to talk Sable into coming to the city for an examination. He said she could help infertile women just by undergoing a few tests. She knew her brothers would never allow it. She didn't even mention it to them.

Jude and Jonas were obsessive when it came to protecting Sable and their sons. They rarely let their little family out of their sight. She thought they were neurotic. If she were Sable, she'd feel smothered, but in some weird way, it all worked for them. She'd never seen three people so in love and so passionate with each other. Watching them together made her jealous as hell. She wanted that for herself. Well, maybe not two men. Just one who made her panties wet would be fine.

She didn't have those kinds of feelings for Roy. She cared about him, but she wasn't head over heels. Maybe she just loved the idea of having a husband and children. God knew, she heard her biological clock ticking, and she wanted a man and a family of her own before she got too old to enjoy them.

Roy might not be her soul mate, but he would provide her with a safe and secure future. If she let him go and then never found love, she could end up alone for the rest of her life. It wasn't a pretty picture. Was there really such a thing as a soul mate? She should stop fantasizing like some teenager and thank her lucky stars for Roy.

"Come on, Janis. Drink up and let's get out of here."

She chugged the rest of her champagne and let Roy lead her to the cloakroom.

* * * *

Janis tried to ignore her neighbors' wild, headboard-banging sex, but every thud made their connecting wall vibrate. She listened to the grunts and groans as long as she could stand it, then she grabbed the alarm clock from her night table and threw it across the room. It hit the wall and slid down to the floor. Not that it would bother the couple on the other side of the wall. They were far too involved in their own pleasure to give a shit about anyone else.

She shouldn't be this frustrated. She'd had a man in her bed for the better part of two hours. Roy had come twice before leaving, whispering something about a lab experiment at the FIRM.

Next door, her neighbor screamed in ecstasy. It didn't seem to bother Roy that she never screamed like that. Despite his determined thrusting, she always had to fake her climax. Did he really accept her faked orgasms as real? Someone who knew so much about a woman's anatomy should be able to recognize a real orgasm.

She never complained, too afraid to find out that he really didn't care about her pleasure. And for sure he'd blame it on her. Tell her she was frigid. She felt like crying. According to the magazines, she should be having multiple orgasms. She couldn't even manage one unless she used her vibrator.

The hell started up again. Next door the headboard thumped a violent, steady rhythm against the wall. The bedsprings creaked, and the moans were louder than ever. No doubt, she'd have to listen to them fuck all night.

She imagined the hot couple, Brad and Angie lookalikes, screwing like Mr. and Mrs. Smith. The pictures in her head excited her more than sex with Roy.

Her breasts ached, and her nipples hardened to tight little points. She slid one hand over her belly to her pussy, already wet and swollen and crying out to be touched. Her finger drew slow circles around her clit. It felt good, but not good enough.

Feeling wicked and wanton, she reached for her trusty rabbit. The ultimate pleasure toy cost seventy-five dollars and was worth every penny.

By now she was soaked, and her vagina swallowed the length of the dildo easily. She teased the rabbit in and out of its hole, while the little ears hummed and vibrated against her clit.

She'd used it so many times she knew the exact position of every button. One touch set the substitute penis rotating.

Her heart rate rose as electric currents gathered and spread. Soon the familiar spasms of her inner walls signaled an approaching orgasm. She didn't want it to end, but there was no stopping it. It was as useless as trying to breathe under water. At some point you had to come up for air. Her legs tensed, her hips bucked, and her inner muscles contracted as if she were trying to milk the cum from a lover's cock.

Oh my God, oh my God, oh my God.

She came down from her high and realized how quiet it had become. At least now she could get some sleep.

Chapter Two

With each determined thrust, the musky scent of sex grew stronger in the small room. A light sheen of sweat covered Noah's upper torso. Long strands of damp black hair clung to his neck and forehead.

Beneath him, Ayala shuddered breathlessly, her body moist and slick against his from their exertions. She tightened her legs around his waist and pushed her hips up to meet his thrusts. As he looked down at her, she let out a breathy hum, and her eyes fluttered shut.

Guilt overwhelmed him. Their kind didn't tire easily, but they felt frustration keenly, and he'd kept her on the edge of a climax over and over again. This time he would let her have her release. Just because he couldn't spill his seed didn't mean he had to torture her.

He lowered his head and used the tip of his tongue to tug at her silver nipple ring. Her eyes flew open and darkened with passion. He took her entire areola in his mouth and played with the ring while he suckled her. Ayala shifted and arched beneath him. Her hands tightened in his hair, and her moans of appreciation grew louder as she urged him on.

"Come with me, Noah," she groaned. Her sweat-soaked body shuddered under his, and he felt her orgasm boil up. Her cunt, hot and tight, embraced his cock in a series of hard contractions.

A sense of being watched came over Noah, and he increased his speed, wanting to perform his duty as well as please the passionate she-wolf. He gave free rein to his imagination and created an elaborate scene in his head. Images of Wade stirred his libido. He imagined Wade's muscular legs resting on his shoulders, pumping into his lover's—

Ayala came with a high-pitched cry that broke his reverie. Any chance of having his own orgasm disappeared. Still, he allowed himself a moment of pride in his performance. Just because he preferred men didn't mean he couldn't satisfy a woman.

When her spasms quieted, her legs released his waist, and she looked up at him with a guilty little smile. "Noah, I—"

He pinched her arm and jerked his head to the side, catching a glimpse of black leather from the corner of his eye. When he rolled off her body, she sat up immediately, bowing her head in submission.

Noah swung his long legs over the side of the bed and acknowledged Alexander with a nod. "Alpha."

Alex approached, exuding the animal magnetism that always made Noah's breath catch in his throat. His leather pants sat low on his hips, and his gauzy white shirt hung open, revealing a hard chest furred with dark hair that trailed enticingly beneath his waistband.

Alex stood next to the bed, so close his leg touched Noah's. He looked down at Ayala. "Did Noah take good care of you, Ayala?"

"Yes, Alpha," she whispered.

Alex raised an eyebrow, his lip curled in a sneer. "I think not, Ayala. What kind of she-wolf are you that you can't get your man to spill his seed inside your cunt?"

Noah saw her lip quiver before she hung her head, letting her long black hair hide her face like a curtain.

"It's not her fault, Alpha," he said quietly.

Alex turned to him. "Yes. It is. She doesn't know how to please you." He ran a hand through Noah's hair, and Noah shivered under his touch. Alex laughed and stroked his hair again. "Go to your room, Ayala. You're of no use here."

Trembling, Ayala got off the bed and gave Alex a wide berth as she left the room.

"I'm not her man, Alex."

"I know whose man you are."

Noah winced at the obvious reference to Wade, the wolf who'd replaced Alex as his lover. "Then why do you keep throwing her at me, Alex?" No one else in the compound would dare call their Alpha by name or question his authority. But he and Alex had a long history together, and when they were alone, Alex permitted him certain liberties.

"We need whelps, Noah. I don't care that you prefer Wade." He frowned then caressed Noah's cheek with his knuckles. "But a union with Wade will not produce a child."

"Neither will a union with Ayala. We've mated many times, and she has yet to conceive."

"Forget Ayala. She's useless. I have an important task for you. One that will conclude with a successful mating."

Noah sighed. Who would Alex pair him with next?

"This one is not for you, Noah. I merely require you to bring her home."

Noah cocked his head, all ears. The ancient cliff dwellings they'd refurbished in New Mexico had been home for more than fifteen years. The setting was far different from the Pine Barrens of New Jersey, where he'd spent his childhood. Nevertheless, he'd come to love their homes, built into the canyon walls using adobe bricks and timbers.

Alex took a photograph from his pocket and handed it to Noah. A woman with long dark hair that wafted in the wind like streamers posed smiling against a forest background.

Noah handed the picture back and shook his head. "Who is she?"

"The mother of my pups."

Noah's jaw dropped. She looked like their women, but that meant nothing. Few of their females had come through the massacre alive. The Gods knew they had been searching for survivors all these years. Noah could count on one hand those that had been found, yet their

Alpha refused to merge their race with the humans. Alex declared he would castrate himself before bedding a human female.

Noah ran a hand through his damp hair. "So you've changed your mind about raising hybrids?"

Alex curled his lip in a snarl. "Of course not. I won't taint our bloodline with half-breeds. This woman is one of ours."

"How can you be sure? There are so few of us left." Noah understood Alex's feelings, even if he didn't always agree with his methods. He shared the Alpha's distrust of humans. He knew all too well what Alex had lost. What they'd all lost.

Their Gods may have chosen the Sacred Lands in the Southeast for their home but when Kweo, the wolf, bedded a human female and created their people, the Lycans fled to the Pine Barrens. Or so the legend said. Much of their history had been lost.

His people lived in peace. When humans settled in the Barrens, the Lycans chose to hide their true identities. They raised their own food and home-schooled their children. But some of the youngsters grew restless and longed to see what lay outside their community. A few left and lived among the humans, lost to the Lycan community forever.

Fifteen years ago, one of their women had married a human. Her parents accepted the man and put their trust in him. When the marriage failed, he betrayed them and came back with others to kill their people and burn their homes. Forest fires were common in the Barrens, and humans didn't cry over dead wolves. No one suspected the true reason for the desolation. The perpetrators kept their silence, most likely afraid of retaliation by any survivors.

And there had been survivors. A small group of shell-shocked youngsters had gotten away, Noah among them. Alex being the oldest, they had all looked to him for leadership. One day he'd celebrated his twenty-first birthday with a wife and child. The next he was a young man leading a group of younger men and a few females halfway across the country. Alex chose New Mexico, hoping their Gods would protect them from further persecution.

Noah was eighteen and became second to Alex. They shared everything, even their bodies, taking comfort in each other during those dark days. Noah fell in love with him, but Alex had sealed off part of himself and didn't allow emotion to affect him or his decisions.

Noah wanted more. He became closer to Wade, who was a year younger, and totally besotted with him. Wade fulfilled his emotional needs and gave him the love that Alex denied him. When the younger man turned eighteen, their emotional connection turned sexual. He'd been afraid to tell Alex, but of course, there was no hiding it. Each left their scent on the other making it obvious to the Alpha that they'd been lovers.

He'd hoped Alex would accept Wade into their sexual union, but the Alpha turned away and ended their physical relationship. He and Wade had been together ever since. He loved Wade, but he still had strong feelings for Alex. Most days he could put them aside, but sometimes they overwhelmed him.

Neither he nor Wade felt the need for female companionship. They remained committed only to each other. But regardless of their preference, the men were compelled to follow Alex's agenda and mate with the pure-bred she-wolves he paired them with.

At first he and Wade found it distasteful to have sex with partners they hadn't chosen. They were a race that had always remained true to their mates.

But family had become a lot more fluid and complex. Due to their dwindling numbers, their women often took multiple husbands or were forced to breed with other wolves if their mates didn't impregnate them. Same sex liaisons were accepted, but the participants were still obligated to breed. It was all for the good of the clan.

"Roy discovered this woman quite by accident. He has no proof, yet, but he feels certain she's one of ours."

Jealousy crept into Noah's chest and circled his heart, squeezing like a snake and spewing venom through his body. Roy had taken Noah's place in Alex's life.

Noah cursed the day Roy had been discovered in Boston. He was smart as a whip and already an undergraduate. Alex lured him to New Mexico with promises of funding further education. He'd done that and more. Although stationed in Philadelphia now, Roy's influence reached back to New Mexico.

"I don't want Roy pursuing this further and jeopardizing his position in the hospital."

Noah turned from Alex's wry smile. He'd never been any good at hiding his feelings from his former lover.

"I hope you can put your dislike for Roy aside. I'm sending you and Wade to Philadelphia. Settle in and meet with Roy. He'll direct you from there. Can you do that?"

"Of course, Alpha."

"Good. I don't want anything to interfere with the capture."

Noah's brow furrowed. "Capture?"

"I want this woman." Alex's face went tight. "Don't let anything stand in your way."

Chapter Three

Wade tried to keep a tight rein on his emotions. They were only renting an apartment after all, but he hated the city, and damn if it didn't feel like he and Noah were making a real commitment to live here. He reminded himself that even though the lease said a year, he and his lover had no intention of remaining in Philadelphia any longer than necessary. Thank the Gods. The concrete jungle freaked him out.

All the upheaval in their lives didn't sit well with Wade. Lately the Alpha's ideas had become intolerable. Even worse, he couldn't share his misgivings with Noah. His lover still had strong feelings for their leader, and anything he said would be construed as jealousy on his part. Which it was.

Noah and Alexander weren't fucking each other, but he knew if the Alpha crooked his little finger, Noah would fall all over himself to jump in his bed.

And being forced to fuck every she-wolf in the compound only added fuel to the fire. He knew Noah didn't have feelings for the women. Neither did he. But he didn't care for the idea of Noah sharing his body with someone else. Wade had lost a lot. He had no intention of losing Noah.

And here they were on a fool's mission, another one of the Alpha's crazy ideas. Not for a minute did he believe they would find a she-wolf. They'd followed too many false leads already. But it was the Alpha's call. He would never pass up the chance to find a female Lycan.

Wade really hoped it wasn't another wild goose chase. If they brought home a she-wolf, then maybe their leader would give them a break.

Unfortunately, he suspected that Roy had concocted the whole thing to gain favor with their Alpha. Roy's jealousy surpassed his own. Although their Alpha had severed his intimate connection with Noah, Roy knew as well as Wade that there were still feelings there, and he didn't like it one bit.

Despite the absence of physical contact whenever Noah and Alexander were in the same room, the atmosphere became so charged they might as well be fucking. Wade had learned to live with it. Alexander had been Noah's first love, and nobody would ever replace him in Noah's affections. Wade considered himself lucky just to be sharing a part of Noah's life.

So they would play out their parts in this charade and let Roy have his moment of glory. For sure he was headed for a downfall when they were unable to track down a she-wolf.

At any rate, their business should be completed quickly. They would find her location, continue their search, and bring her home. Or as he expected, they would uncover a fraud and go home. Either way they would soon be home and that's all he cared about. He missed the vast open space and solitude of New Mexico.

Fifteen years ago he'd left the only home he'd ever known and followed the Alpha to New Mexico. Back then he'd just been Alex, a young man who had lost more than most of them. Wade had watched him cry over the bodies of his mate and baby son. Then Alex had gathered their small band of survivors and whatever they could carry and led them away. They never looked back. There was nothing left to see. And he never saw Alex cry again. He was a strong leader, and they owed him their lives, but he'd been damaged beyond repair.

Wade snuck a peek at Noah. Nothing ruffled him, at least not so it showed. Noah had deep feelings, but he projected a calm exterior, no matter what. Sometimes Wade wondered if he knew the real Noah.

It didn't matter. What he knew, he loved. There was no one else he'd rather be with. The man was more than his best friend and lover. He was the closest thing to a soul-mate he'd ever have. The only person in the world he could really trust.

The woman across the desk cleared her throat, and Wade tried to focus on business.

"I really need references." She looked straight at Noah, who had been handling their business arrangements so far.

Janis Outlaw intrigued him. He didn't know any females outside his community, and Ms. Outlaw's shaggy blonde designer haircut and wide-set blue eyes were in complete contrast to the women back home. Most of them had obsidian eyes and long, coal black hair.

Her fair coloring made her seen fragile and in need of protection, even though she tried to look so business-like and confident in her gray suit and high-necked white blouse. Another difference. Lycan women weren't involved in business of any kind. Their only concern was making babies.

The woman shifted in her seat. Spots of color highlighted her high cheekbones. Wade's nostrils flared. He sniffed the air. Her scent gave her away. She was interested in more than business. Her delicate musk sent out a message that seemed to be directed at Noah. She was aroused.

His lip curled in response. She was barking up the wrong tree. Noah was his. He had no interest in females of any kind. Wade's only competition was their Alpha, and that was long over.

He looked over at his lover and frowned. Noah's eyes were focused on the woman. Even though Noah feigned interest, Wade couldn't suppress a stab of jealousy. He reached over and laid a possessive hand on Noah's arm.

Noah ignored the gesture, but it didn't escape the woman. She looked down at his hand then up at his face. Her blue eyes assessed him frankly, and she smiled, almost regretfully.

"About the references," Wade said. "We're new in town, but we'll both be working with Dr. Roy Granger at Philadelphia Hospital."

Ms. Outlaw's eyes widened. "Well, in that case there's no problem. I know Dr. Granger." She pushed a printed document towards him.

"You'll both have to sign the lease," she said. "And I'll need the first month's rent and two months for a security deposit."

Wade wondered briefly about the connection between Ms. Outlaw and Roy, then her eyes, the darkest, most striking blue he'd ever seen, caught his and he lost his train of thought.

"I hope this is okay." Noah pushed a wad of cash across the desk, and those hypnotic eyes turned to him. Noah flashed his most disarming smile. "We haven't had a chance to open a bank account yet." Noah could be charming when he wanted. Wade knew that first hand.

"Oh, it's no problem." The woman lost a bit of her composure as she picked up the money. She took a set of keys from her drawer and handed them to Noah. He touched her fingers and kept the connection a beat too long. The woman flushed darker, and her scent ripened.

"I hope you're both very happy here." She looked from Noah to him. "If you need anything just call. Or stop in."

Wade smiled politely, but he doubted he'd be happy until he returned home again.

* * * *

Noah looked around the empty apartment. Gods, he wished he were home. He felt closed in, suffocated. He glanced at Wade. "You shouldn't have told the rental agent we're working with Roy. There's not supposed to be any connection between us and him."

Wade didn't reply. He stared at Noah insolently from across the room.

"What's wrong?" Noah asked him.

"You flirted with that woman."

Noah laughed. "So what?"

"She was aroused. I could smell her musk as if I had my nose in her cunt."

Noah walked over to his lover and put his arms around him. "I can't help it if I'm irresistible." He nuzzled Wade's ear.

Wade sighed. "I wish we were home. I think the Alpha is dead wrong about—"

Noah cut off his words with a gentle kiss. The last thing he wanted to do was argue about Alex. Wade parted his lips, letting Noah possess his mouth, and Noah slipped his tongue inside. Noah's breath caught when Wade sucked on it in a parody of what was to come. Noah deepened the kiss, then pulled back and nipped Wade's lower lip. "I'm really glad you're here."

Wade leaned his forehead against Noah's. "Even though I screwed up and mentioned Roy's name?"

"Can we not talk about Roy? He's an asshole."

"Fine with me. I can think of better things to do." Wade backed him against the wall. He grinned wickedly as he knelt at Noah's feet.

Noah went commando, and his cock strained at the fabric of his slacks. Wade watched the growing bulge and rubbed it through his trousers.

"Hell, Wade. You can do better than that," Noah groaned.

Wade looked up at him and licked his lips. "Beg me."

Noah looked down at him through narrowed eyes. "Please, please, please suck my cock, Wade."

"Well, since you asked so nicely." He unzipped Noah's trousers, and his cock sprang free, long, hard and aching for attention. Noah sighed and leaned back against the wall in anticipation.

Wade gripped the base of his shaft and stroked him a few times. Then he used his tongue on the sensitive ridge of the cockhead.

"Gods, you know that drives me crazy," Noah muttered.

Wade laughed. "That's the idea, lover."

Wade's talented tongue found the underside of his balls and licked straight up to the tip of his cock, where he tongued the slit to catch a drop of pre-cum.

Noah tensed and tried to thrust in his partner's mouth, but Wade backed off. "Dammit, Wade. Stop teasing me."

"I want to feel your bare ass." Wade unbuttoned Noah's slacks and tugged them over his hips. He caressed Noah's thighs before cupping his buttocks and sliding his mouth over his partner's hot swollen shaft.

Noah felt Wade's throat close around him. His knees buckled, and he put his palms flat against the wall. "Gods," Noah groaned. "Your mouth feels so fucking good."

Wade hummed around his erection, then released him and looked up with heavy lidded eyes. "Tell me again what you want," he murmured in a husky whisper.

"Dammit! You know what I want." Noah growled. "I want to come."

Wade sighed throatily. "Get down here and tell me."

Noah kicked his slacks aside and tore off his shirt on the way down. He helped Wade get out of his clothes and then he lay on his side facing Wade's crotch.

Wade already had Noah's dick in his mouth. "Fuck, that's good," Noah murmured thickly. He bent his top leg to give Wade better access. Then he slipped an arm under Wade's bottom leg and pulled him closer so he could lick and suck his balls. He wrapped his lips around Wade's swollen cockhead and sucked, pulling the foreskin down and then up the shaft, flicking the tip with his tongue.

Wade made unintelligible noises around his cock, which only aroused him more. Noah gasped. Shit, he was too damn close, and he wanted to make sure Wade was with him. He gripped Wade's cock and squeezed the base of his shaft, stroking and pumping in rhythm with his sucking.

The only sounds in the room were wet sucking noises and grunts of encouragement. They had done this so many times before. Each knew exactly what the other needed.

Wade's body tensed, and his balls drew up tight. He shuddered and jerked with his release. Noah swallowed spurts of semen and felt his own orgasm coming like a runaway train.

His hips bucked, and Noah abandoned control. He groaned in blissful agony as Wade sucked him dry.

For a few minutes they lay sated and spent. Then Noah turned his body around and pulled Wade in for a passionate kiss.

"That was really nice," Wade murmured against his mouth.

"You're the best," Noah whispered. "Baby, you blow me away."

Chapter Four

Noah could find his way anywhere in the Gila Forest, but here in the city, he was lost. Even if he'd visited the hospital before, which he hadn't, he'd never be able to track it by scent.

His sensitive nose balked at the toxic fumes of car exhaust, garbage in alleyways, and the unwashed bodies of the homeless who warmed themselves on street vents. The urban rankness overwhelmed him. Everything he saw, smelled, or touched made him long for the unspoiled terrain of home. From desert to rugged mountains to deep canyons, his adopted land offered his people the solitude and escape they desired.

Sighing, he stopped to consult his street map. Annoyed pedestrians jostled him as they tried to reach their destinations, all of them so focused on their own wants they didn't even try to avoid a collision. Noah stood his ground, and a few of the humans looked up, surprised that he didn't give an inch.

Noah ignored them all, intent on his own business. He found a hospital icon on the map, and he realized they were closer than he'd first thought. He took off without a word, knowing Wade would follow. They covered the few blocks in silence.

A brick and wrought iron fence surrounded a quadrangle of four large buildings. Even if there hadn't been a sign proclaiming the Foundation for Infertility and Reproductive Medicine in big black letters, he'd have no trouble identifying the FIRM. The modern façade was in complete contrast to the older brick buildings in the complex.

Noah gave their names to a redheaded woman at the reception desk. She told them to have a seat and then she disappeared through another door.

Wade frowned at him. "What are you so pissed about?"

"I'm not looking forward to our meeting with Roy."

"I'm sorry I made things more difficult."

"It's not you," Noah said through clenched teeth. "He just rubs me the wrong way."

"Do you want me to beat him up for you?" Wade said, a perfectly serious look on his face.

Noah's eyes narrowed, and then he laughed. "No thanks, slugger. He might kill you, and I'd miss your blowjobs."

Wade smiled and put a hand on his knee. "Well, if you change your mind, just let me know."

The woman returned, and Wade quickly removed his hand. They both rose and followed her into Roy's office. She slipped out and shut the door behind her.

Roy looked nothing like the Lycan Noah remembered. His tan had faded, and he wore his dark hair short. The toned body he'd shown off at home was now covered up with khakis, button-down shirt and lab coat. He looked almost human sitting behind his modern desk, surrounded by cherry wood and leather.

Roy gestured to two chairs. "It's been a long time."

Not long enough. "It looks like you've embraced your new life," Noah replied as he and Wade took seats.

Roy's face hardened. "I've adapted for the sake of my work. I have every intention of returning home when I'm done here. Make no mistake about that."

Noah smiled tightly. Roy harbored some jealousy over Noah's past with Alex, and he obviously wasn't happy about the distance between him and the Alpha.

"I only meant that your guise is quite convincing. If I couldn't smell your true nature, I'd believe you were human myself." He knew Roy wouldn't take it as a compliment.

Roy's eyes turned cold. "I do what I have to, for the good of the clan. I expect you'll do the same."

"Of course." Noah meant it. No matter what, the preservation of their people remained their most important objective.

"Good." Roy slid a photo across his desk.

Wade spoke for the first time. "We've seen this. She looks like our women, but it doesn't prove anything."

Roy didn't spare Wade a glance. "Can't you keep a leash on your boy, Noah?"

Noah clenched his hands but ignored the comment. "Where did you get the picture, Roy?"

"From Janis Outlaw."

Noah and Wade exchanged a look that didn't go unnoticed by Roy.

"Yes. Your landlady. Why do you think you were told to go to that particular building? You did rent an apartment?"

"Yes."

"And you're settled in?"

"What's to settle?" Noah asked. "We travel light, and we sleep on the floor." The landlady was definitely not one of theirs. How did she figure into this? "How is Janis Outlaw involved?"

"Her family lives in Black Wolf Gorge, a small town in the Pennsylvania Wilds. Last year one of her brothers moved here for a short time. He was brought to the ER after being stabbed outside a bar. At the time Janis was seeing an ER doctor, and he admitted her brother for a few days, even though he wasn't that badly hurt. I suspect Janis wanted him to dry out. The man's an alcoholic."

Noah glanced at Wade. "Can you get to the point, Roy?"

Roy settled back in his chair and narrowed his eyes at Noah. "I'm giving you background information. Focus, Noah. There's nothing more important on your agenda than this. Alex wants all your attention on the matter at hand."

Noah's nostrils flared. That Roy called the Alpha by name wasn't lost on him. Evidently Roy had risen in stature and ingratiated himself with Alex. The thought of Roy and Alex together made him ill. The fact that he'd done the same thing to Alex when he took Wade as his lover didn't make it any easier to accept. Noah kept his face a composed mask. He refused to give Roy the satisfaction of knowing he'd struck a nerve.

Roy waited a minute to let his words sink in then he continued. "A few weeks later I ran into Janis' ex-boyfriend, and he shared an interesting story with me. Her brother went back home and entered into an unconventional relationship with his twin and a woman. The woman gave birth to twins."

Wade crossed and uncrossed his legs. He tapped a foot on the floor. Noah suspected he did it solely to annoy Roy.

Roy paused. He waited until he had their complete attention before he continued. "Having twins is not that unusual. Having twins, each fathered by a different man, is."

Now Roy had his attention. Wade's too. His partner sat forward in his chair, all ears.

"Heteropaternal superfecundation is the medical term. The woman releases multiple eggs during ovulation and mates with more than one man within a short period of time. Rare in the human world. Not so rare in the animal kingdom. In fact, it's very common in dogs. Strays have been known to produce litters in which every pup is from a different father. Years ago, before our people were slaughtered, I witnessed this phenomenon in my own family. Of course my interest was piqued."

"And you confirmed that the twins have different fathers?" Noah asked.

"As much as I was able. I took advantage of the fact that Janis had broken up with the doctor. I saw her on the pretext of looking for a new apartment, and I asked her to dinner. We've been dating ever since. She discussed her family with me, and I urged her to have her sister-in-law come in for a workup. Janis told me there's already been DNA testing. One of the brothers is a biologist."

"Where did you get the photo?" Noah asked.

"I took it from her apartment, had copies made, and returned it. Everything fits. Her family lives in a forested area. Just the place a she-wolf would hide out. My instincts tell me she's one of ours. Find out what you can from Janis. Then track the woman. Of course I would like you to keep the fact that you know me from Janis."

Noah jumped in before Wade could say anything. Roy already had little confidence in Wade. Better to take the blame for this on himself. "It's too late for that. I slipped up and told her we had jobs waiting for us here."

"That was stupid," Roy snarled. "Keep my name out of it when you see her again. If she asks, tell her the positions here were already filled."

Noah thought they'd already seen the last of their landlady. Now it looked like they'd be paying her a visit. "How do you know the woman in the picture isn't human? You said this does happen in the human population."

"That's your job, Noah. Sniff her out. Once you find her, you'll have no trouble identifying her."

"And if she is one of ours?"

"Then bring her in."

Bile rose in Noah's throat. The woman had children and mates. She wouldn't come willingly.

* * * *

Janis tried to concentrate on paperwork and failed miserably. Last night she'd put a face on her dream lover, two faces in fact. Both of her new tenants played starring roles in her erotic fantasy.

For the first time she could imagine herself in Sable's position, a woman with two gorgeous men fulfilling her every sexual desire.

Of course her tenants wouldn't look twice at her. Two drop-dead gorgeous men walk into her office and they turn out to be gay. She was sure of it. It was something in the possessive way that Wade looked at Noah, the way he'd laid a hand on Noah's arm. Life was so unfair.

Unfortunately, it just added to the allure. Knowing they were off-limits made them ten times more desirable.

But it was more than just wanting something she knew she couldn't have. Chemistry was involved here, that magnetic pull that only happened with certain men. She'd never felt it with Roy. But as soon as Noah and Wade walked through her door, butterflies migrated from her stomach to her chest, and nervous jitters took over. Suddenly she felt flustered and couldn't string a few words together to form a coherent sentence. Hopefully, she'd covered it well.

She'd focused on one, then the other. They were similar in looks with their black hair and those topaz eyes that reminded her so much of Sable's.

Looking at Wade, her heart thumped against her ribs. When she'd turned to Noah, just the sight of him made her panties wet. Both men attracted her equally. How freaky was that?

She tried to picture them together, two naked, sweaty males doing whatever men did to each other. Blowjobs for sure. She wasn't totally unfamiliar with the ways men satisfied each other.

She'd watched porn before. Hell, she had twin brothers who left their movies and magazines all over the house while they were growing up. Their taste ran to two guys with a woman. Fancy that. Ironic, they both ended up with the same woman.

But watching two men with another woman, she'd always been distracted by the female presence. Checking out the competition overshadowed the sensuality of the scene. She'd always preferred watching the physical contact between the men.

Now, if she was the woman enjoying their attentions, that would be different. It intrigued her and intimidated her. Men always seemed to know how to satisfy other men. Could a woman really know a man that intimately? Please him that completely? She wouldn't mind finding out.

She imagined herself between these two men, her mouth on Noah's cock, Wade kneeling behind her. He'd be fingering her pussy and telling her what his lover needed to get off.

Four hands touching her, two mouths kissing her. What would it feel like to have two cocks fucking her? Her panties were soaked through and through just thinking about it. She'd never have to buy another battery for the rabbit.

Janis fanned herself with a folder and tried to come back to the boring reality of work. Her concentration gone, she gave up. She'd already wasted the entire morning daydreaming impossible scenarios. She might as well go to lunch.

Janis had dressed carefully that morning. She wouldn't admit it to herself, but she wanted to look nice in case she ran into Noah and Wade. Instead of her usual business suit, she'd selected a dress, something that exposed a bit more flesh. Low cut, sleeveless and midnight-green, it set off her blonde hair. Wearing a revealing dress in the winter wasn't the sanest or most sensible idea she'd ever come up with. It might be okay for a party but not for work. But with the right accessories, a dress could easily go from evening wear to office wear. A fitted jade cardigan made all the difference and still revealed her ample cleavage. A pair of high-heeled pumps completed the look.

Of course she hadn't seen the men, and now, she was all dressed up with nowhere to go. No point letting it all go to waste. She already had a man. She might as well give him the benefit of her makeover.

She grabbed her purse and coat before she could change her mind and headed over to the FIRM. Hopefully Roy wasn't busy and she could persuade him to take her to lunch. Mooning over two gay men when she had a boyfriend was stupid.

She entered the building and went straight to Roy's office. The front room was empty. Damn, had she missed him? She could check the cafeteria, but she decided to try the door to his inner sanctum first. The knob turned, and she walked in.

Roy sat behind his desk. He turned to her, looking for all the world like the proverbial deer frozen in headlights. He composed himself quickly. She really had surprised him.

She approached the desk. "I'm glad you're here. I thought I'd come by and take you to lunch."

"I, uh, I'm really tied up now, Janis," Roy stammered.

Smiling, Janis put her hands on the edge of his desk and leaned over to kiss him. "I'm glad I caught you." She also caught a flash of red hair from the corner of her eye and looked down in horror.

The red-haired bitch was on her knees under the desk, sucking Roy's stiff cock. It looked like she had most of it stuffed down her throat. She hoped the slut choked on it.

For once Roy was speechless. So was she. Her fingers closed around the first thing they felt, and she threw it at the woman, wishing she'd grabbed something heavier than a mouse. The bitch released Roy's dick with a soft pop. The bastard didn't even lose his erection.

Janis turned abruptly and stomped out. She slammed the door behind her and crossed the reception area. She almost made it out to the street, but Roy grabbed her arm and pulled her back.

She yanked it away. "How did you get your pants zipped up so fast, you lying son of a bitch! You must get a lot of practice. This is the woman who means nothing to you."

Roy looked around, more worried about who might overhear than about her feelings. "I didn't lie. She doesn't mean a thing to me."

"She was on her knees in front of you. What do you call that?"

"A blowjob."

"You bastard!"

Roy shrugged. "What's the big deal? We never had an exclusive relationship. And you don't like to suck cock. She does."

Janis slapped him hard. She put everything into it, but he didn't even flinch.

He laughed at her. "I guess this means you don't want to see me tonight?"

Chapter Five

Janis gave off an anxious vibe. Noah's acute senses picked up on it immediately.

"How did you know where I live?" She played with a loose thread at the edge of her sweater.

He smiled reassuringly. "Your name is on the mailbox." He hoped she wasn't afraid to let them in. Two six foot, four inch men could be intimidating. Maybe tonight wasn't the best time to get better acquainted. She'd be more approachable in her office.

Janis let out a shaky laugh. "Oh, of course."

Noah debated putting this visit off for another day, but she invited them in before he could make up his mind. Relieved, he followed her inside. He and Wade were anxious to conclude their business here and move on.

"Sit down," Janis said. "Would you like something to drink?"

"No. Thank you." Noah hesitated. "Actually, we stopped by to invite you to dinner."

"Noah and I thought you might clue us in on life in the big city," Wade added. "You know, direct us to the best places to buy furniture. That kind of thing."

Janis's eyes appeared red. She looked like she'd been crying. "I'm sorry. Maybe another time. I'm afraid I wouldn't be very good company tonight."

Noah's mind raced with possibilities. A distressed woman would be easier to manipulate. If he and Wade turned on their wolfish charm and gained her confidence, they might find out more. Even bed her if it came to that. It wouldn't be the first time they fucked for the good of the clan. Surprised, Noah found himself thinking that fucking Ms. Outlaw would not be a hardship.

"It might help to talk about it," Noah prodded.

"I don't think so." Janis shook her head.

Wade caught her attention. "Why don't we have that drink after all?"

"Wine okay?" Janis asked.

"That would be great."

Janis disappeared into the kitchen and returned with a bottle of Merlot and three wine glasses.

Noah opened the bottle and filled the glasses to the rim. Wade lifted his in a toast. "To new friends."

"And hopefully new job opportunities." Noah added, hoping to put distance between them and Roy.

Janis frowned. "I thought you'd be working with Roy Granger?"

"So did we. Unfortunately, when we saw Dr. Granger today he informed us that the positions were cut because of budget concerns."

"Son of a bitch." Janis muttered under her breath.

Noah's brows arched in surprise. "It won't affect our lease will it? We have enough money to cover our rent."

"No. It's not that." She took a big swallow from her glass. "You're not the only ones who got screwed today. So did I. And not in a good way."

What had Roy done now? Noah felt his gorge rise. He exchanged a look with Wade.

"Sorry." Janis flushed scarlet. "I'm just so angry. Roy and I had been dating. Today I went to his office, intending to ask him to lunch, and I caught him with his pants down. Literally." She downed the rest of the wine. "And his slut of a secretary on her knees under the desk."

There was a moment of stunned silence then Noah threw back his head and laughed. Wade followed, and Janis soon joined in.

Noah regained control first. Wade actually had tears running down his cheeks, and Janis hugged her ribs as if she had a stitch in her side.

Wade wiped his face with the back of a hand. "I'm sorry. I'm not laughing at you. I got this picture in my head, and Roy is just such a pompous ass..."

"He's a jerk," Noah added. "And that redhead doesn't hold a candle to you. You're well rid of him." He found he really meant it. Roy was a fool. If he wanted a woman's company, he couldn't do better than Janis. Oddly enough it pleased him that they'd had a falling out.

Janis' extraordinary eyes sparkled. "All of a sudden I'm hungry. How about a pizza?"

* * * *

Janis collected the dirty plates and put them in the sink. "I'm glad we didn't go out. I enjoyed this."

"Me, too." Noah stood to give her a hand.

"You bought the pizza, I'll clean up. Put some music on, or pick out a movie. The DVDs are in the cabinet under the TV."

While Wade went through the movies, Noah walked around the living room, taking in everything at a glance. The furniture was comfortable, mission oak. He didn't see many personal touches other than a display of photographs on a console table. One, in particular, caught his eye.

He was looking at it when Janis walked back in the room.

"Those are my nephews." Her voice took on a wistful tone that touched Noah.

"They're beautiful children," Noah said. "And the woman?"

"My sister-in-law. Their mother."

"Really? They don't look anything like her." This photo didn't have the red-eye effect. The woman's distinctive golden eyes seemed to be looking into Noah's. The hair on the back of his neck stood on end.

Janis took the picture and handed him another. "The twins take after their dads."

"Dads?" He studied the blond men, posed shirtless in the sun. They were tall, good-looking humans with muscular bodies. He and Wade could subdue them easily.

"My brothers. Fraternal twins just like the babies." Janis laughed. "Well, not exactly like the babies."

Noah planted a puzzled expression on his face. "I don't understand."

"I don't really understand it all myself." Janis said. "They each fathered one of the twins. Evidently Sable released multiple eggs and had sex with both of them."

"Sable?" Noah rolled it around on his tongue. It was first time he'd heard her referred to by name. He racked his memory. Had he known a Sable in his childhood?

"Yes. She's wife to both of them."

"Rather unconventional," Noah murmured. Although he and Noah were forced to mate with the she-wolves, they'd never shared a woman. The idea appealed to him.

"It works for them."

"How do you feel about that?" Noah murmured. "Do you disapprove?"

"Not at all. They're happy. That's the important thing."

"Do you think you could do that? Make love to two men, I mean?" Noah looked at her through slitted eyes. The familiar tightening in his groin surprised him. His cock had grown hard.

Janis flushed red. "I don't know that she makes love to both at the same time. It's really none of my business."

"I didn't ask about her. I asked about you." She might think it none of her business, but the scent of her arousal told him the idea intrigued her. Her reactions intrigued him.

Janis's navy eyes opened wide. Her musky scent deepened and tickled his nostrils. Noah's lips curled in a self-satisfied smile.

From the corner of his eye, he spied Wade frowning. Did his harmless flirting make Wade jealous? It was only business, he told himself.

Except he enjoyed it way too much. Her natural scent, unconcealed by flowery cologne, tied him up in knots. It was like nothing else he'd ever experienced. Where Wade and Alex tantalized his senses with their masculine animal scents, hers was rich and succulent. It flowed through his body like thick warm honey, settling in his cock and crystallizing to a diamond hardness.

Awareness sparked between them. His gaze locked on hers in a smoldering stare that neither could break. He caught Wade's movement behind her. His lover shocked the hell out of him when he put his hands on Janis's hips. Had their arousal sparked his?

The idea of having Janis sandwiched between him and his lover grew and tantalized him with possibilities. Desire slammed into him, and an edgy animal hunger took over his body. He suppressed a growl and fought the urge to shift. His wolf protested like a randy dog, but deferred to his human side.

Janis seemed incapable of movement. Noah held her gaze, and electricity sparked between them, charging the air with static energy.

Details imprinted on his mind—the curve of her jaw, her eyes like sapphires against her pale skin, a tiny beauty mark at the corner of one eye. The tip of her tongue appeared and swiped her lips. God, he wanted to lick those velvety lips. Her earthy scent grew stronger, and Noah's cock lengthened against the zipper of his slacks.

Time seemed to stand still. Noah desperately wanted to know how it would feel to be intimate with a female he really desired, but he would never take a woman by force. He waited, hoping for a sign from Janis.

* * * *

Janis's breath hitched, and she shuddered. Did they really mean to seduce her? At five-ten, Janis found there were few men that towered over her like Wade and Noah did. It was an incredible turn-on to feel small and helpless between these two sexy men. The desire to explore her dark fantasy took hold, but her insecurity held her back. Would they find her wanting like Roy obviously did? Suddenly, she didn't care. Maybe it was the wine. Maybe she needed an ego boost. Whatever the reason, she wanted this experience.

"I don't know." She stared into Noah's eyes. "I never had the opportunity before."

"What if you had it now?" Wade murmured in her ear. His warm breath made goose bumps rise on her skin. He licked her ear and nuzzled her neck.

Noah moved closer and put his hands on her hips. He and Wade kissed over her shoulder.

"Oh." She felt their kiss down to her toes. Noah's cock pressed against her aching pussy. Wade rubbed his growing erection against her ass.

Noah pulled away from Wade, and his lips searched for hers. She put her arms around him and deepened the kiss, then pulled back. Janis had never felt so much, or wanted so much, from the touch of someone's mouth on hers.

"Do you want this, Janis?" Noah said softly against her lips. "Do you want us?"

"I do," she said. The hell with Roy and his redheaded nympho. Having these two men in her bed would go a long way toward erasing the humiliation he'd put her through. She leaned her head back and looked at Noah seriously. "But, do you really want this?"

Noah rubbed his hard cock against her. "What do you think?"

"I don't know what to think," she said hoarsely. "I thought you were gay."

Noah smiled. His eyes looked past her at Wade. "We don't label ourselves with society's titles. We are what we are. We want what we want. Right now we want you."

Janis breath caught in her throat when she saw the dark promise in his eyes. Already she was so wet and hot for him, for them, that she felt herself coming undone. "Yes," she hissed, then twisted her head toward Wade. "Yes, Wade."

Wade moved around to her side and kissed her. For a moment their tongues danced then he came up for air.

"I've never done this before," Janis told him. "I don't know how to please you."

Wade chuckled. "Then it will be so much fun teaching you how." He went to his knees before Noah and unzipped his slacks. Noah's cock sprang free, long, thick and inches from Wade's face. She'd never seen an uncircumcised penis before.

She watched transfixed as Wade stroked him, and the foreskin moved back and forth over the head of his cock. She bit her lip. Her fingers itched to touch him.

Janis tensed along with Noah when Wade cupped his balls and lapped at the pre-cum leaking from the tip of his penis. Noah groaned and twisted his fingers in Wade's hair. Curiosity and lust kept her rooted to the spot. This was nothing like the X-rated movies she'd seen. These men really cared about each other. It made all the difference.

She wanted to be Wade, to touch Noah like he did. The power and passion these two men displayed was palpable. The strong masculine electricity that flowed between them sparked a fire in her belly. She'd never seen anything so hot and so sexy in her life. Her breasts felt achy and heavy, and her panties were soaked. She squeezed her thighs together, but it did nothing to assuage the throbbing between her legs.

She'd never enjoyed sucking Roy's cock, but right now, all she wanted was to get to her knees in front of Noah and take him in her mouth, taste him.

Wade released Noah and looked up at Janis. "Come here."

She got to her knees beside Wade, and he kissed her. Noah's taste exploded on her tongue. She grabbed Wade's head and sucked on his tongue, wanting more. Wade pulled back and nipped her bottom lip. He held her gaze. "She likes your taste, Noah. And I think she wants to suck your cock."

"Do you, Janis?" Noah asked as he removed his clothes.

She whimpered and reached for him, but Wade held her back. She stilled as Wade removed her sweater, then unzipped the back of her dress and pulled it over her shoulders.

"Very pretty." Wade played with the lace on her bra before unhooking it. "But you look much prettier without it." He tossed it aside. "Lift your hips." He got rid of her dress and panties then got out of his own clothes.

Completely bare to their eyes, she had a moment of hesitation, but when she saw the naked desire in their gaze, it disappeared.

"Up on your knees," Wade said.

She complied immediately. Noah's rock hard erection tempted her. Like a woman in a dream, Janis rubbed her cheek over the velvet skin of his cock and moaned in appreciation.

Wade took her hand and wrapped her fingers around Noah's shaft. Then he got behind her and covered her with his body like a mantle. He put his hand over hers and showed her how to stroke Noah and push the silky foreskin all the way back.

"What are you thinking, Janis?" he said in her ear.

"How much I want Noah's long, beautiful cock inside me."

Did I really say that?

Wade chuckled. "Later." His big, warm hands cupped her breasts. It felt so good, she stopped and turned her head to search for his lips.

Wade whispered in her ear. "Don't stop. I want you to suck Noah's cock while I touch you."

Janis moaned in her heat.

She took Noah in her mouth and sucked gently.

"More, Janis." Noah twisted his hands in her hair.

"Curl your lips over your teeth. Just slightly," Wade said. "Tease him with your tongue. Flick it across the tip as you suck."

"Gods, that feels good," Noah groaned.

Wade squeezed her breasts and pinched her nipples. "Good girl."

Janis moaned around Noah's cock.

"How does that feel, Noah? Do you like what she's doing to you? Does she suck your cock better than I do?"

"Not better." Noah groaned and cupped the back of her head, rocking his hips. "Different. Incredible."

Knowing how much Noah liked this turned her on. Excited, she sucked harder, wanting to be the one to make him come.

"Slow down. He'll come much too fast."

Noah growled in frustration as Janis released his cock. She looked up at him, alarmed.

Wade laughed. "His bark is worse than his bite. He really loves to be teased." Wade turned her head and captured her mouth for a kiss. "Hmm. I can taste Noah on you," he murmured as he slid his hand between her thighs. "Gods, you are so wet." He slipped a finger inside her, then another. "I think our girl needs some attention."

Janis whimpered and pushed against his hand.

He finger fucked her for a few seconds, and she felt the first fluttering ripples of an orgasm.

"Oh my God! Don't stop," she cried.

"I won't," Wade murmured in her ear, his warm breath fanning the flames of desire. He cupped a breast with one hand, and the other moved between her legs. His thumb teased her clit until her body quivered.

Janis let out a throaty groan, and her thighs clamped down on Wade's hand as her release spiraled out of control. He held her close until her body stilled.

Janis leaned her head back against Wade and looked up at Noah. His eyes were so dilated they looked black. An ache started in her belly again, and she let out a whimper.

"I think we need to take her to bed, Noah." Wade stood, pulling Janis up with him. He lifted her off her feet and carried her to the bedroom.

Wade set her on the bed and followed her down. Noah joined them. He rolled her to her side and kissed her until she melted against his heat. She purred deep in her chest when she felt Wade's warm body press against her back, his stiff cock rubbing against the crease of her ass.

Is this how they planned to take her? Wade buried in her ass and Noah in her pussy? She'd dreamed about it, wanted it. She couldn't believe it was really going to happen. She squirmed and wiggled between them.

Noah slid down her body, trailing kisses and swirling his tongue around her navel.

"Please," she whimpered.

"Please what?" Noah looked up at her.

"I need more."

"You heard her, Wade."

Wade sat, pulling her up with him. He leaned back against the headboard, and Janis rested her back against him. Wade spread her long legs with his and caressed her breasts.

"Jesus." She threw her head back against his shoulder.

Noah crept between her legs and lowered his head to her pussy. He spread her open with his thumbs, and his long tongue swiped her slit from bottom to top.

"Yes." Janis gasped. It felt so damn good. She tried to arch her hips, but Wade held them still with an iron grip.

"Don't let her come yet," Wade muttered harshly. Noah looked up, his eyes locked on Wade's. "I want to be inside her."

Janis moaned. "Condoms. Bathroom."

Noah sighed, but he made a quick trip to the bathroom. He returned with a handful of condoms, and she watched him tear one open and roll the latex over his lover's penis. It was incredibly sexy.

He grabbed her waist and lifted her while Wade guided his cock to her entrance and pushed the tip inside. Noah's hands on her hips pushed down and impaled her on Wade's cock. Her head rolled back against him, and she made unintelligible animal noises. She barely heard Noah's voice, encouraging her on. "Please, please, please," she begged them.

"How does she feel?" Noah asked Wade.

"So good," he groaned.

Noah's fingers parted her labia, and he licked around Wade's cock where it disappeared inside her pussy. When he nuzzled Wade's groin and licked his balls, Janis grabbed his hair and tried to move his head back where she wanted him.

Noah traced slow circles around her clit as she moved on Wade. She lifted her arms, twined them around Wade's neck, and pressed back against him.

"Fuck, Noah. I'm close," Wade grunted.

Noah sucked her clit into his mouth. Something clenched inside her, and she arched her back. She cried out, and Wade held her through wave after wave of shuddering contractions.

Noah squeezed Wade's balls as he rose to his knees and kissed him, sandwiching Janis between them.

Wade gave one last thrust up and shuddered with his own release.

She finally opened her eyes and saw Noah staring at her. Her gaze locked with his, and some understanding passed between them. She felt Wade stirring behind her.

"Let me up." Wade kissed her shoulder. "I'll get Noah off."

Noah's passionate stare bored into her soul. "I want Janis."

His words made her shiver. Molten heat pooled in her belly again.

Noah lay back, pulling her down on top of him. She rubbed her hips against his while he kissed her.

"I want to fuck you."

"Yes," she hissed. She wanted Noah, needed him desperately. She took a condom from Wade, opened it and smoothed it over Noah's very stiff prick. Then she straddled his hips and guided him inside her. He felt so good, she hardly noticed Wade get off the bed.

The mattress shifted as Wade settled in behind her. His hands rubbed circles on her ass and pushed her farther down on Noah's cock, making them both moan.

She felt something cool between the cheeks of her ass, and she went rigid when Wade's finger pressed against her tiny hole.

"Relax, sweetheart. I won't hurt you." Wade leaned over and kissed her shoulders, her back. "I want to be inside you with Noah. I want to feel his cock while I fuck you. Tell me you want us both."

"Yes," she moaned.

"Yes what, Janis?" Wade pressed.

"Yes, please fuck me, Wade. I need you both," she whimpered.

Noah pulled her down, giving Wade access. She gasped when his finger slipped past the tight ring of muscle.

Noah whispered encouragement while Wade slid a second finger inside and stretched her.

"Are you ready, sweetheart?" Wade murmured.

"God, yes," she hissed, as the head of his cock nudged her opening. Every slow push drew another moan while the men told her how beautiful she was, how good she felt.

The burn turned to pleasure, and she pressed back against Wade. "Oh, God, Wade. More."

Wade stopped, and Noah started moving. He took control from beneath them. Wade adjusted his tempo to Noah's, and Janis was content to follow their leads. The men moved in tandem, and the musky scent of their coupling grew stronger with each synchronized thrust.

The feeling of being filled so completely was new and exciting. She'd never felt so connected to anyone as she did with these two men. The heat built between them, and she teetered on the edge of a climax.

"I'm close," Noah said harshly.

Wade grunted. He reached around Janis and rubbed her clit. Her muscles contracted around the thick cocks inside her. She felt the men tense.

"Fuck!" Noah shouted. He and Wade thrust hard and deep. Wade growled and leaned over her back. He sank his teeth in her left shoulder, and Noah bit down on the right.

Janis threw her head back and screamed, feeling their orgasms as acutely as her own.

Chapter Six

Noah woke first. He rubbed the sleep out of his eyes and looked at Janis sandwiched between him and Wade. His mark on her shoulder stood out against her pale skin. Confused thoughts whirled in his brain.

Lycans were territorial by nature but he'd never felt the need to leave a mark on Wade. Nor had Wade ever left one on him. Yet it had seemed so natural to brand Janis.

The woman was smart and funny and easy to be with. And so responsive to him and Wade. The sex had been phenomenal. No pressure to perform, no worries about reproducing. Maybe being with a female he liked and felt comfortable with brought out some inborn Lycan instinct to claim a woman.

He thought about Roy and Janis together. Maybe his dislike of the man made him want to leave a mark on Janis. A no trespassing sign? Absurd. What did he care if Janis saw Roy again? More likely, petty jealousy led to it. A message to his rival—you might have Alex, but I had something that belonged to you.

Wade's eyes opened, and he sat up. He looked at Janis, then Noah, and shrugged.

A fleeting thought crossed Noah's mind. Would he and Wade have the same relationship after this? The three of them together set off an explosion of feeling that took him higher than ever before. Would it be as good between them without Janis? It had to be, because they were never going to see her again. This was a one-time only fuck. He tried to put it out of his head. They'd learned all they could here. It was time to go. The sooner, the better.

* * * *

When Janis woke, the men were gone, leaving only the heady scent of their sex behind. She felt lonely and bereft without them, but she wasn't surprised. They had each other. She was only a diversion. She never expected to be a permanent part of their relationship. Still, she expected to see them again. Probably for lunch since they hadn't gotten around to discussing furniture.

She showered and slipped on a blue dress, the same shade as her eyes. Then she grabbed her purse and headed downstairs to make coffee in her office. Sitting in the lonely apartment didn't appeal to her.

As soon as she entered the office, she saw the paper on the floor. She knew immediately who had slipped it under her door, and she felt a cold chill go up her spine.

Sorry we had to leave so quickly—something came up back home. W & N

Her heart sank. Not even a *thanks for a great night* or a *call you* at the end. Definitely a kiss-off. It wouldn't surprise her if they never came back.

It hurt that they didn't want to see her again, but she didn't regret one minute of last night. It had been wonderful. A once in a lifetime fling that erotic fantasies were made of. It all seemed like a dream anyway. Well, it would fuel her dreams for many nights to come. And she knew one thing for sure, she'd had the best sex of her life and she'd never settle for anything less again.

Janis tried to lose herself in work, but she felt lonely and at odds. She didn't want to be here. Suddenly she wanted her family. She picked up the phone and felt better immediately when Sable answered.

* * * *

"Home is where the hearth is," quipped Janis as she poked at the logs in the fireplace. Yesterday she'd been in the city. Today she was in a totally different world. It felt good to be back.

Jude smiled indulgently. "I've missed you, but not your puns."

"And I've missed you. All of you. Especially these little guys." She looked down at the twins, sleeping peacefully in a crib that now occupied a permanent space in the den. A stab of envy hit her.

Would she ever have a child? Her biological clock sounded louder than Big Ben. She reached down and caressed each downy head. Undisturbed, the babies snored softly. It wasn't fair. Sable had two. Why couldn't she have one of her own?

"They changed my life," Jonas said. "Added something that I never knew I was missing until they came along."

"You're very lucky." She actually got misty eyed. These two beautiful boys had changed both of her brothers. Or maybe it was Sable's doing. She'd never seen either of them so happy and content.

Jonas stood and came up behind her. He put his arms around her and squeezed. "If you moved back home, you wouldn't have to miss us."

Janis squirmed out of his hold, turned and narrowed her eyes at him. "Jonas, have you forgotten it was you who sent me to Philadelphia in the first place?" Her twin brothers were younger than her, but Jonas had always been the one to take charge.

"It was only supposed to be temporary. You did a great job handling the settlement and managing the building, but now I can hire someone to look after things."

"It's been six months. I've made friends—"

"You have friends here who miss you."

"Jonas, you don't understand," Janis protested. "I like what I'm doing." How could she tell him that she wanted what he had, and if she couldn't have it, then she needed to bury herself in work? What else did she have in her life? "I'm going back to school. I intend to get my real estate license. I love you all, but I don't want to come home and be chief cook and bottle washer."

Sable guffawed. "Little chance of that. I've inherited your job."

Both Jonas and Jude turned and stared at Sable with stricken faces. She jumped up and went to one, then the other. "And there's nothing else I'd rather be doing." She looked at Janis. "I just meant that you'd be free to do what you want. As long as you gave me a hand with the babies once in awhile."

"That would be a labor of love." Janis smiled at Sable. "There's just more opportunity for me in the city. And I've grown to like the hustle and bustle."

"To each his own," Jude said. "Do you want a drink? Jonas and I have become teetotalers. Hard to believe, I know."

"Not at all. You don't need it. You both look like you're high on life. I guess this unconventional lifestyle agrees with you."

Jonas looked at his twin brother before responding. Jude stared back and gave Jonas the smallest shake of his head.

What silent message had passed between them? Her curiosity piqued, Janis forced herself to keep her mouth shut. Evidently she wasn't privy to some secret they shared. Oh well, she had her own secrets now. She wasn't about to reveal a thing about her ménage. What happened in Philly stayed in Philly.

"We're very happy," Jonas answered at last.

"And so am I," added Sable. "Doubly happy."

Janis sighed. "Two babies and two men. I don't think I could manage it."

Sable pulled both men into a group hug. "It's amazing what you can do when you're in love. I'm very lucky."

"So are they," Janis added.

"I'm glad you think so, Janis. I was afraid you wouldn't approve of our relationship."

"Are you kidding? I was at your wedding. Remember?"

"Yes. But I married Jude that day. You had no idea that I was also in love with Jonas."

"Hey, I don't blame you. My brothers are gorgeous." Janis stopped smiling as thoughts of Wade and Noah crossed her mind. Unfortunately, Sable looked enough like them to be their sister. She was a constant reminder of Janis's one night of lust.

"Seriously, Sable. I've never seen them happier, and that's good enough for me." She almost opened up about Wade and Noah. She thought she could put that night behind her, but she couldn't get the men out of her head or her heart. Her family would surely understand. But something held her back. Maybe it was because she knew she probably wouldn't see them again. It was humiliating to admit to her family that she'd been so wanton with two strange men. And for what? A one night stand. It wasn't the love story that Sable shared with Jude and Jonas. "Besides, I finally have the sister I always wanted. And two beautiful nephews that I'm crazy about."

"And I finally have a family."

Wow. Sable looked like she wanted to cry. It might be time to change the subject. Sable didn't talk much about her family. Jonas had told her they were all dead and she had a hard time dealing with it, so Janis usually steered clear of the subject. "You must be superwoman," she joked.

"Sex is great exercise." Jude winked at Jonas. "And exercise keeps you fit and wanting more sex."

"It's a vicious circle," Jonas agreed.

"I'll keep that in mind," Janis responded dryly.

* * * *

Janis shooed everyone out of the kitchen. Sable had cooked an excellent meal, grilled venison and mashed potatoes. It was only fair that she clean up while the devoted parents took care of her nephews. She didn't mind. In reality she wanted a little time alone.

Coming home had become an overwhelming experience. She hadn't expected such strong feelings of jealousy to overtake her. It seemed that being with Wade and Noah had only made things worse. Now that she knew what it felt like to be with two men that she really desired, she wanted more. She wanted what Sable had, men who loved her and a family of her own.

She'd always wondered how Jude dealt with the jealousy issue. After all, he married Sable first. But seeing Wade and Noah together made her realize that men who were secure in themselves and their partner wouldn't have those issues.

Her heart sank. It might be time to accept the fact that she'd never have that kind of relationship. That she might not have a relationship at all. At least she had her work and classes. And she could still have a child. Maybe she would adopt a baby one day.

Janis put the last of the flatware in the dishwasher and stood. She glanced out the small window over the sink, and her eyes went wide.

Two pairs of golden eyes stared back at her. A full moon spotlighted the scene. Wolves.

She knew what a wolf looked like. A pack had been relocated and housed at the Black Wolf refuge for several years before wolves were taken off the Endangered Species List. Then the men, her brothers among them, declared open season and hunted the pack to extinction. There hadn't been a wolf sighting in the area for many months. Where had these animals come from?

They held her gaze for a few heart-pounding seconds, then heads hanging low, the animals trotted off.

Janis's parents had been killed by wolves when she and her brothers were children. They'd been raised by their paternal grandparents, who had instilled a fierce hatred of the animals in all three of them. She screamed for her brothers.

They came running, Sable behind them. Jude reached her first. He grabbed her by the shoulders. "What the hell happened, Janis?"

"Wolves," she whispered. She pointed to the window with a shaky hand.

Jude looked out the window. "There's nothing there."

"There are no wolves around here anymore," Jonas added.

"You probably saw wild dogs. Maybe a coyote." Jude rubbed her back. "You've been living in the city too long. You're not used to having animals around anymore."

"I know what I saw." She hugged her middle to calm herself.

Jude sighed. "All right, we'll take a look."

"You better take your rifle," Janis warned him.

"Right." Jude turned to Jonas. "I'll grab my rifle and meet you out front.

"Don't use it unless you have to, Jude." Sable looked anxious.

Janis stared at her. She had the distinct impression Sable was more worried about the wolves than the men.

* * * *

A real feeling of dread hung over Sable as she followed her husbands outside. Janis grew up here. She knew what a wolf looked like. And the scent was wrong. What if it wasn't just a timber wolf that wondered onto their property? If Malcolm had come here in wolf form, it could only mean trouble.

The men got down on their knees and inspected the ground outside the kitchen window.

Jude looked up at her. "Whatever it was didn't leave prints. They walked on the stones around the flower beds."

Jonas stood and put his arms around her. "We'll look around the house and make sure everything's okay."

Sable hugged him. "Be careful. Only shoot to defend yourself. It could have been Malcolm."

Jude stood, and the men framed her between them. Jude looked doubtful. "What would Malcolm be doing here at this time of night?"

"And Janis says she saw two of them. Whatever they were," Jonas added.

"I know it's not likely but please be careful." Their friend and neighbor, Malcolm Connor, was the only other wolf-shifter alive, besides herself. They had both survived the massacre of their people and only recently found each other. At first Sable thought Malcolm would be her mate, but he fell in love with a human female. He and Karin were happy together, and they had a child.

Until recently her husbands had been enemies with Malcolm. Now they accepted him as family. His half-Lycan son would grow up with Max and Sam. The children wouldn't be alone in the human world. If anything happened to him…

"Stay here," Jude told her. "We'll be right back."

Sable didn't move until they returned. She breathed a sigh of relief when they told her they hadn't seen anything.

Chapter Seven

Noah led the way back to the sheltered clearing where they'd left their clothes. They shifted to human form, and he dug through the leaves he'd used to cover their garments. "We should have been more careful. I didn't want anyone to see us. Now they'll be keeping a closer eye on the grounds."

Wade shrugged. "What could we do? We needed to get close enough to verify the scent was hers and not some feral animal. What do you think? Are you sure she's one of ours?"

"I'd stake my life on it." Her distinctive Lycan scent, unnoticeable to humans, convinced him. And they'd caught a glimpse of her through a window. No question the woman was a she-wolf, a real beauty, even better-looking in person.

"So you agree with the Alpha that she belongs with us?" Wade asked, an uncertain tone in his voice.

"I don't know. I don't like breaking up a family. It doesn't feel right to me."

"I've been thinking the same thing. And when I smelled Janis and saw her inside the house it made it worse."

"I never expected her to be here. It complicates things. One more person we have to worry about."

"Noah, when I saw her, I couldn't help staring. I wanted to reach out and touch her. I've been hard ever since." Wade wrapped his fingers around his erection.

"You're acting like a young pup." Noah scolded Wade, but he felt the same. Seeing Janis again brought back sweet memories of the night they spent together and a longing to recapture those feelings. It sounded like Wade felt the same. Bedding Janis may have started out as part of a plan to get information, but it ended up adding a whole new dimension to their relationship.

He'd been arrogant enough to think he was master of his own destiny, but maybe the Gods had other plans. They'd put a woman in his path who turned him hard with one toss of her golden locks. But why a human woman? Are we meant to mix our bloodlines after all? It didn't matter now. If Janis knew what they were about to do, she would despise them. And they couldn't let their personal feelings interfere with their duty to the pack. "This fascination with a human female is going to get us into serious trouble."

Wade stood abruptly. His stiff posture gave away his anger. "Her name is Janis. Are you saying you don't have feelings for her?

Noah sighed. Wade had deep emotions. That's why Noah had fallen in love with him in the first place. He'd always told Wade that he could confide anything to him. How could he expect his lover to bury those feelings now? "I do care for Janis. But our feelings don't matter, Wade. She's a human, not one of us. And if she ever found out what we're doing, she'd hate us."

Noah stood and squeezed Wade's muscled shoulder. He fumbled for the right words. "We made a mistake. Got too caught up in the moment. We had sex. That's all." Who was he trying to convince? Wade or himself? Underneath the lust he felt for Janis were feelings of affection and protectiveness. Things a wolf felt for his mate. It confused him. He'd never wanted or needed a woman before.

Wade broke into his thoughts. "Whatever I feel doesn't take away from what I have with you. It only adds to it."

Noah smiled at him. "I don't doubt your commitment to me. I just want us to get through this safely and go home. For good or bad, we cast our lot with the Alpha. That means no consorting with the enemy. We stick to business, and we stick with our own kind."

"I know. We already lost one home. I don't want to lose another."

"Good, then we're in agreement." A woman, especially a human, would only complicate their lives. He and Wade shared the lust and the emotion without the perplexing entanglements that a woman always brought to a relationship. Besides Wade knew him better than he knew himself. No woman could satisfy him more, physically or emotionally.

Even now, just looking at Wade's hard muscular body in the moonlight made him salivate. The Lycan looked like a sex god. Noah focused on the light dusting of dark hair that covered Wade's pecs. He licked his lips, and his eyes burned a path down the treasure trail that led to Wade's penis.

Wade's cock grew thicker and harder under his scrutiny, and the foreskin rolled back exposing the swollen helmet head. Noah swallowed hard when Wade slid a hand between his thighs and rolled his balls in his palm.

Wade's eyes were heavily hooded with desire. The intensity of his gaze made Noah's pulse quicken. His partner started to jack off, slow and easy.

Noah reached down and took his own cock in hand. Moisture gathered at the tip, and he spread it over the mushroom head with his thumb. He stroked his dick, matching his tempo with Wade's lazy rhythm.

Wade moaned, and Noah tasted blood. Without realizing it, he'd bitten through his bottom lip. His cock throbbed, and his hand moved with a will of its own, pumping harder and faster from base to tip. His hips bucked as he pushed against his fist. Through glazed eyes he watched Wade do the same.

Wade worked his cock faster. His hand was a blur. He let out a growl and then a howl of release.

Noah felt on the verge of his own release. Perspiration poured down his body. His stomach clenched, and his breathing turned coarse and ragged. His cock writhed in his fist like a hot, living thing, driving his lust higher. A primal drumbeat pounded in his head.

He imagined himself gripping Wade's hips and thrusting deep inside his ass. His balls tightened as he relinquished control. A white hot light burned behind his eyelids. Noah groaned with sweet satisfaction and called out Wade's name. Streams of hot cum spurted over his hand and belly.

Noah sank to the dirt, closed his eyes, and lay on his back, panting softly. In a moment Wade's warm breath caressed his neck. Wade kissed his throat and licked a path to his ear.

"I love you, Noah," he whispered. "I hope you know that."

"I do, and I feel the same. The sooner we get back home, and back to our lives, the better."

"Good." Wade squeezed his thigh. "We'll get through this. Do you have a plan? It won't be easy getting the she-wolf out. The men are always around her. And now there's Janis to worry about."

Noah had been thinking the same thing. But there were horses and other animals on the ranch. Surely the men took care of them while Sable stayed inside with the babies. "I'm hoping an opportunity presents itself where the men are working the ranch. And if it doesn't, well, I think we can subdue two human men with no problem. It's the woman I'm concerned about. A she-wolf will fight to the death for her cubs."

"We have to drug her," Wade said. "There's no way around it. Maybe the men and Janis as well. I don't want to hurt them."

"And you think I do? What do you take me for? This whole thing stinks. I've no love for humans, but I'm beginning to think some of our own are worse.

"The Alpha?"

"Was never like this before. He's changed. I think Roy's poisoned him against everyone."

"That wouldn't have happened if I hadn't come between you."

"It's not your fault. He couldn't give me what I needed. And he could have joined with us. He chose not to. That's all water under the bridge now. It is what it is." Noah sighed. "We watch and wait until the right time presents itself."

"I think we should take the babies with us," Wade said.

"Her whelps weren't included in the plans. The Alpha won't be happy."

"I don't care. I can't separate a mother and her children."

"I don't want to do it either." Noah thought about it for minute. "Okay. We take them. I'll tell him she's more manageable knowing we have possession of her sons."

Wade nodded and retrieved their clothes.

They were far outside the town limits, and they had a long walk ahead of them to the Black Wolf Inn. Noah would have preferred living in the rough, but Wade convinced him it would be more dangerous than living in town. If they were spotted as wolves, every hunter in the area would be looking for them. Now he was afraid that would come to pass anyway.

And staying in town was starting to look even riskier. They'd never expected Janis to be here. They had false IDs, but what if she spotted them in their human forms? How could they explain their presence in the small town? They needed to complete their business fast and get back to New Mexico. At least they were both in agreement about that.

With their long muscular legs and powerful strides they made good time on the return trip, and before long, they had the inn in their sights. Built in the early nineteen hundreds with hand-hewn logs, it presented an imposing façade.

A tin roof sheltered a porch lined with rockers. The men stepped up, and Noah tried the front door, half afraid they'd been locked out. The door opened easily, and they walked inside.

Noah had hoped that the combination lobby and great room would be empty. No such luck.

Two men sat in front of the massive stone fireplace where embers still smoldered in the hearth. A bottle of whiskey and a checkerboard sat on the long wood plank table between them. The innkeeper looked up from his game and scowled at them.

His suspicious nature didn't surprise Noah. People in small towns were always wary of strangers. He just hoped the man hadn't found evidence of Wade sleeping in his room. The Black Wolf Lodge had ten sparsely furnished but impeccably clean rooms. They had booked two, but only used one.

Tongues wagged freely in a small community. If people knew they were lovers, it would only make them more conspicuous.

Noah nodded and kept walking, but the innkeeper's grim face and cool stare followed them. They'd almost reached the staircase when the man's question stopped them in their tracks.

"You boys taking in a little night air?"

"Just a walk." No sense lying. The only place still open was the tavern, and it would be easy enough to find out they hadn't been in there.

"Best stay indoors. It's safer."

Had they just been threatened? No. His imagination was getting the best of him. This whole mission freaked him out. He just wanted it over and done.

Chapter Eight

"Are you sure you don't need me?" Jude must have asked Sable the same question six times.

"I always need you, baby." Sable batted her eyes at him. "Now go take care of your horses."

"Blech!" Janis pretended to stick a finger down her throat and gag. "How do you stand him?"

"He's cute," Sable said.

Jude made a face at Janis. He walked over to Sable and put his arms around her. "You sure? I'll stick around if you want me to."

Sable hugged him, and Janis watched them suck face. A tiny pang of regret pierced her heart. She wondered if Noah and Wade had concluded their business at home and returned to the apartment. Or had she really seen the last of them.

Jude came up for air and wiggled his hips against Sable's.

Sable gave him a little shove. "Down, boy. Now I know why you want to hang around here."

He laughed and swatted her butt.

"Wow. That was some kiss." Janis fanned her face with her hand. "Sable, I swear you put my brothers under a magic spell."

Sable laughed. "Horndogs! Both of them." She winked at Jude. "Use up some of that energy on the horses. Go on. Don't you have enough to do without worrying about me?"

"How many horses do you have stabled?" Janis asked, curious.

"Too many," Sable said. "Eleven horses are too much for one man to take care of."

"One man?" Janis echoed. Her brothers offered boarding and stud service in addition to taking care of their own animals. They'd always hired extra help if they needed it.

"Jonas is busy in his lab." Jude's voice took on a defensive tone. "He's working on selective breeding. He says eventually we'll have the best horses in the state."

"If you live that long." Sable's brow furrowed.

"So why not hire some help?" Janis asked.

"I like doing things my own way." Jude got that bulldog expression on his face, and Janis knew there was no changing his mind.

She suspected her brother's desire for privacy had a lot to do with their unusual marriage. She was sure they didn't want their business all over town. Gossip ran wild in Black Wolf, and her brothers wouldn't want Sable or the boys harassed.

"I'll help you." The words were out of Janis's mouth before she even realized she'd said them.

Jude looked at her like she was crazy. "You never liked working in the stable when you lived here."

"But I did it when I had to. I know how to take care of horses."

Jude shook his head adamantly. "Stay here and help Sable."

Sable put her hands on her hips. "I don't need any help. You do. If Janis doesn't mind, I think it's a great idea."

"Okay you're outvoted here," Janis said. "Let's do it. We'll get finished twice as fast."

Jude hesitated then shrugged. "Okay then." His eyes locked on Sable. "I'll have my cell. If you need me, call."

"Yeah, yeah." Sable started to wipe down the kitchen table.

Janis and Jude stopped in the den to take a peek at the babies in their crib. The boys were sound asleep, so cute in their matching jammies that Janis was tempted to wake them for some playtime. But Jude shushed her. There'd be plenty of time to play later. They headed for the stables.

* * * *

The wolves crouched among the densely packed pine trees and kept their eyes trained on the house. When Janis exited with one of the men, they exchanged looks of understanding. Noah watched the two humans disappear in the direction of the stable, and he nodded.

Only the she-wolf and her other mate remained in the house. They might not get another chance like this. It was now or never.

Noah picked up a small canvas bag with his teeth and tore off. Wade followed close on his heels. They made for a copse at the back of the house and shifted. Wade stretched and gave Noah a dark look. Noah didn't like this anymore than his lover, but they couldn't back out now.

The padlock on the unused back gate had been cut two nights ago. Noah gripped the bag in his hand, and they slipped through the gate and around the house. Their point of entry would be a low window in the den.

Noah took his tools out of the bag. Using a diamond glass cutter and a suction cup, he made a fist-sized hole in the glass. Then he reached inside and unlatched the window.

As stealthy in their human bodies as their animal ones, they climbed through the window. Noah looked at Wade. He held a finger to his lips and pointed first to the sleeping babies and then to the window. Wade nodded in understanding, and Noah removed a chloroform-soaked cloth from the canvas bag and moved toward the arched entry that led to the foyer.

Across the foyer, the living room was empty. So was the adjoining dining room. But he spied the black-haired she-wolf in the kitchen. She stood at the sink with her back to him.

Knowing she'd smell him as well as the anesthetic, Noah moved in on her fast. He knew the moment she sensed him. Her back went rigid. As quick as he was, she'd already turned, snarling and snapping as he reached her.

Noah slammed her body back against the sink. Her face contorted, her fangs already extending. Panting like a rabid dog, she raked her lengthening claws across his cheek. Noah bent her back and slammed the chloroformed rag over her face. She fought like the devil, but finally, her hold loosened, her hands flopped at her sides, and the claws receded.

Noah kept her body anchored to the sink with his and removed the cloth from her face. Her head wobbled on her neck while her eyes, heavy-lidded and glazed, tried to focus on him. Her chin hit her chest, then her head jerked back, and she remained motionless. Noah lifted her effortlessly and carried her to the den.

Wade was already gone. Evidently the twins had been a handful. The tools were still where he'd left them. Noah put everything in the bag and climbed through the window, the she-wolf in his arms.

He followed Wade's trail, smiling when he saw his lover trying to calm two angry babies. "Not much of a mother, are you?"

Wade scowled. "Want to trade?"

Noah laid Sable on the grass. "Give them here." He reached out for the twins and set them down next to their mother for a few minutes. It calmed them down. He looked up at Wade and smirked. "You carry the she-wolf."

The men moved swiftly, and the babies seemed to enjoy their trip through the woods. The chill didn't seem to bother the little half-breeds. They might be blond and blue-eyed, but they definitely had a wolfish side to them.

The men reached the spot where they'd left their clothes and an ATV. Noah gave each boy a bottle to suck on while they dressed. Sable remained limp and unconscious. Wade sat with her and the babies while Noah took the wheel. He drove through water wherever he could to hide their trail.

When they were miles away, he finally allowed himself a sigh of relief. "Call Roy," he said to Wade. "Tell him we have the cargo."

Wade's side of the short conversation was a series of yeses and nos. "There's a small private plane waiting for us at Hangar D," he told Noah. "And the Alpha will have a car waiting at the airport when we arrive home." He hesitated. "If we get home."

"We will," Noah assured him. "We move a lot faster than they do, and if we're lucky, they won't discover she's gone for hours. We already have a big head start, and I'm covering our trail as best I can. Hopefully, it will go cold by the time they start looking, and we'll already be home."

Chapter Nine

Janis remembered why she hated working in the stable. The smell of hay and horseshit clung to her, and she hadn't been this tired in a long time. They'd been at it for hours. The horses were groomed and checked for cuts, swelling and loose horseshoes. Their hooves were picked to remove rocks and mud from the soles. They were fed and watered. And then Jude had the nerve to ask if she wanted to ride.

"Hell no!"

"Just kidding." Jude laughed, and she started to laugh too.

"All I want is a hot bath and a nap."

"Go back then. We're almost done here."

"Well, if you're sure you don't need me anymore." Janis started backing away before he could change his mind.

"City living made a wimp out of you." Jude's laugh followed her out of the stable.

Janis could barely put one foot in front of the other. The walk to the house seemed much longer than it had that morning. Feeling like a zombie moving in slow motion, she pulled a key out of the pocket of her jeans and unlocked the front door.

It would be nice to see the boys, but not smelling like a horse. She threw off her old sheepskin jacket and headed for the stairs, already imagining the hot water cascading over her aching body.

She took two steps and sniffed. A strange new smell overpowered the stink of horseshit. Curious, she descended the steps and followed the sickly sweet odor to the kitchen.

The smell was stronger. Dirty breakfast dishes were still in the sink. Janis frowned. Sable never left the kitchen dirty.

She walked into the den. The boys were not in the crib, and she turned away. A chill blew into the room. She knew Sable was hot-blooded, but this was ridiculous. She turned back to shut the window.

It wasn't open. She looked closer, and a chill that had nothing to do with the weather ran down her spine. She let out a cry and ran for the stairs to find Jonas.

* * * *

By the time Jude got back to the house, she and Jonas had already gone through every floor. They were back in the den when Jude ran in, wild-eyed. Janis pointed at the window.

"Fuck! Fuck! Fuck!" Jude bent over, hands on knees, and took big gulping breaths of air. "This is my fault. I should have stayed in."

"What could you have done?" Jonas asked tightly. "They used chloroform. They would have knocked you out. Maybe even killed you."

"Oh Christ." Jude groaned. "The babies."

No one bothered to answer. What was there to say? Janis looked at her brothers and started crying. Their tanned faces appeared ashen. They looked like they wanted to cry too.

"You didn't see anyone at all when you came back from the stable?" Jude's hands were shaking.

Janis shook her head. "I was about to go upstairs for a shower when I smelled something weird. That's when I looked around and found where the window had been cut. Did you see anything outside?"

"I took a quick look coming back from the stable," Jude said. "The back gate was open, the padlock cut. I think we should take Sherlock and see if we can pick up a trail."

"Oh God," Janis moaned. Kidnapped. Right under their noses. "I'll wait here for the sheriff."

The two men looked at each other but didn't answer.

Janis wiped her eyes with her arm. "You did call him, didn't you?"

Jude looked at Jonas. "We're not calling the sheriff. We're not calling anybody."

Janis narrowed her eyes at Jude. "We need to organize a search party."

"Sit down, Janis." Jude sat and patted the couch next to him.

Janis felt dread in every part of her body. What the hell was going on?

"Sable is very special." Jude took her hand. "The boys too. Nobody can find out how special."

"Sable is a Lycan," Jonas broke in. "She can shift into a wolf. Nobody—"

Janis started laughing hysterically. More from fear and disbelief than amusement. "A wolf? Like the ones who killed our parents?"

"No. Not a feral beast. A person who can turn into a wolf. A Lycan," Jude said. "I saw her change in the woods, and we trapped her." He winced and looked down shamefaced. "We wanted to breed her and—"

"Are you saying my nephews are the result of some kind of crazy experiment?"

"God no! It's not like that, Janis. We fell in love with her." Jonas sat on her other side. "And she fell in love with us. This three-way marriage. It wasn't unusual for her people." Jonas reached out for her.

Janis raised a hand to ward him off. "Supposing I did believe all this, and I don't, why can't we call for help?"

"If anyone finds out what she is, they'll want to study her and the boys, or worse. I'm afraid that's why they were taken." Jude explained all this as if he really believed it. She'd have to humor her brothers, but they still needed help.

"Surely there's someone we can go to for help," Janis cried.

"There might be one person." Jonas looked over at Jude. "Malcolm Connor."

"Why him?" Janis asked. There'd always been bad blood between Malcolm and Jude. It was only since her brothers married Sable that the two families became closer. And that was only because Sable was friends with Malcolm and his wife Karin. They had a son just a few months older than her nephews.

"Tell her," Jude urged. "We have no choice now."

"Janis, swear you won't breathe a word of any of this."

"Of course."

"Malcolm is like Sable."

"A Lycan," she said indulgently.

"Yes. One of the few survivors of his people. Like Sable. If anyone can help us, it's him."

* * * *

Janis didn't know the Connors well. She actually knew Karin's mother better than Karin. Grace lived in Philadelphia, and she'd taken in Sable as a houseguest for a time. Janis and Grace had planned the wedding for Sable and Jude.

Of course, at the time, Janis hadn't known that Sable was actually hiding from her brothers. Evidently Jude tracked her down, and when he found out she was pregnant, he asked her to marry him. Then Jonas had to be convinced that they were meant to be a triad. No wonder he'd been drinking. These three had already been through hell and now this. It wasn't fair.

They all sat around Karin's kitchen table, a bottle of whiskey and glasses in front of them. Malcolm paced back and forth like a six foot four bear. His face was truly scary to look at. Janis could almost believe he really was a Lycan.

"We're wasting time sitting here," Jude complained. "We need to start tracking them."

"Let me think for a minute," Malcolm snarled.

"Okay. While you think, I'll go back and get Sherlock."

"You don't need the bloodhound." Malcolm stopped short. "They're probably already out of town, out of the state even." Four stricken faces looked back at him. "They're okay. I'm sure of it. Someone found out who they were and took them, but they're worth more alive than dead."

Janis moaned, and Karin came over to hug her. "Don't worry. Malcolm will find them."

"I sure as hell will," Malcolm growled. "I'm going out to track them as far as I can. I can learn a lot just from their trail."

"We're going with you." Jonas was already rising out of his seat.

"Oh, no you're not. I can make better time myself."

Jude got up angrily. "I'm the best damn tracker in the county."

Malcolm laughed at him. "Oh, you think so." He started to unbutton his shirt. "Listen to me. I want them back as much as you do, and I will get them back. Make no mistake about it. But right now I want you here protecting my wife and son, who might be next on the list. As soon as I have something to go on, I'll be back."

Janis watched fascinated as Malcolm pulled down his jeans. He went commando, and his cock was impressive even in its flaccid state. Tall, dark, chiseled face. Why did everyone remind her of Wade and Noah?

Malcolm's face contorted, and all thoughts of her tenants fled. Gray hair spread from his shortened feet up his legs. His spine bent, and he went to all fours. Popping, like the amplified cracking of hundreds of knuckles, made her cover her ears with her hands. A massive gray wolf crouched where Malcolm had once stood. Janis got up and backed away in fear. "Oh my God." Was this one of the animals she'd seen outside the kitchen window?

"It's okay." Karin came to her. "Don't be afraid."

Malcolm approached and sat a foot away. Karin got to her knees and put her arms around him. She looked up at Janis. "He's still Malcolm."

Janis crouched down beside her. If this animal could find Sable and her nephews, she would embrace it.

The wolf turned its yellow eyes on her, and for a second, she froze. "You were outside the house a few nights ago. With another wolf."

The wolf shook its massive head back and forth.

"It wasn't Malcolm," Karin said. "Maybe some of the pack survived. Or…" She looked in Malcolm's eyes. "Could there be others out there like you and Sable?"

Malcolm let out a warning growl and went to the window. He leaped over the sill and disappeared.

Chapter Ten

Sable tried to escape the murky depths of the river and rise to the surface. The feeling of being submerged for a long stretch of time frightened her. She'd been trapped underwater without oxygen for too long, and she struggled to suck in air.

Consciousness came with a fit of coughing. Sable sat up and fought for control. She heard her own intake of breath between each scream she let out.

The door of her small adobe prison opened, and a tall, dark man entered. She saw him through a haze of tears, and she wiped her arm across her eyes to get a better look. He smelled nothing like the wolf who'd taken her captive.

"Where are my babies?" Her throat felt raw, and her voice came out a croak.

The Lycan approached the bed and stood looking down at her. She pulled the cover up over her naked body.

"All in good time," the wolf told her. The mattress shifted under his weight.

Sable snarled and bared her teeth at him. She wouldn't kill him until she knew where he'd hidden her cubs.

He laughed. "I can see it will be fun taming you."

Sable started to shift. Through the haze of her anger, she heard his warning.

"Shift and you'll never see them again."

She stopped immediately and stared at him, body tense, muscles quivering.

He smiled. "I see my man was right to bring the half-breeds. I have no use for them, but if you behave, I'll let them live."

Sable gasped and clenched her fists. "Who are you?" she growled.

"I'm your Alpha."

"I don't have an Alpha."

"You do now, and you'll follow the rules of the pack."

"The pack? Where am I?"

"You're home." He reached out and cupped her cheek. "Where you belong."

Sable slapped his hand away.

The Lycan snarled and twisted his hand in her long hair. He pulled her head close. "Don't ever do that again." His eyes glowed with red-hot anger. "Ayala!" he screamed, and a trembling young woman entered with Sam and Max wiggling in her arms. As soon as they saw Sable, they reached their little fists out and started crying.

Sable let out a whimper and made a move toward them, but the wolf had her firmly by the hair. "Let me go," she cried.

"You'll have many more. You won't miss them."

"No!" she screamed. The other woman cowered and wouldn't look at her.

"Look at me." He grabbed Sable's chin and held her face steady. "I'm going to tell you this one more time. Do as I tell you, and I'll let them live."

Sable nodded, and he released her. She looked at her twins then back at him. "I'll do whatever you say."

* * * *

For a minute Janis had no idea where she was. The bedroom was smaller than hers at the Outlaw ranch. She sat up, and her head pounded. Then she remembered. She was in the spare bedroom at the Connors' house.

They'd talked for hours. Her brothers weren't crazy. She'd seen Malcolm change to a wolf in front of her eyes. Her sister-in-law could do the same thing. Her nephews might be able to as well. They wouldn't know for sure until puberty.

Jude and Jonas were afraid she would feel differently about Sable and their children. That's why they hadn't confided in her before. She tried to convince them that her feelings hadn't changed, but inside she wasn't really sure.

Karin had suggested they all try to get some rest until Malcolm returned. Janis didn't think she'd sleep, but she wanted some time alone to think. She couldn't process it all. Too much had happened in a short time. Evidently she had fallen asleep.

She turned to check the alarm clock on the nightstand. It was only ten at night. She hadn't been out long. She got up and went into the adjoining bathroom to pee and wash her face. Then she walked out to find her brothers and see if there was any word from Malcolm.

Karin had provided pillows and blankets, and Jude and Jonas had sacked out on sofas in the great room. They weren't asleep. As soon as they heard her, they both sat up. She felt so sorry for them. They looked exhausted, haggard—worried.

Just then, Ralf let out a howl and ran to the window. Janis jumped when the gray wolf leaped through it a few seconds later. A light came on, and Karin descended the steps from the loft.

Everyone still had their jeans on, except Malcolm who was now standing naked in front of the stone fireplace. Karin grabbed his jeans from a kitchen chair where he'd left them and handed them to him.

"Did you find anything?" Jude asked anxiously.

"Enough." He kissed Karin. "Can you make some coffee, honey?"

She nodded and went to the kitchen. Malcolm followed her and sat at the table. So did everyone else.

He looked at Janis. "You say you saw wolves the other night?"

"Yes. Two of them."

He shook his head. "It was wolves that took them."

"How can you be sure?" Jonas asked him. Everyone looked at each other stunned.

"I'm sure because I scented them. They're Lycan." Malcolm looked around the table. "I want you all to think real hard. Did anything else unusual happen? Anything concerning Sable and the boys?"

Jude had his head in his hands. "Nothing."

Jonas groaned. "No. I can't think of a thing."

Malcolm looked at Janis. "Janis? Anything at all? Here or in Philadelphia?"

She bit her lip. Surely Wade and Noah had nothing to do with this. She really didn't want to talk about them.

Malcolm prodded her. "Even something that seems insignificant might turn out to be a big help."

"Two new tenants rented an apartment. Two men."

"What did they look like?" Malcolm asked quietly.

"Oh, God. They looked like you," Janis cried. "And Sable. I remember thinking they had her eyes."

"Did you see them again, talk to them?"

She looked at him stricken. "We spent the night together."

Jude started to rise. "Janis—"

"Sit down." Malcolm waved him down. "It's okay. We don't need all the details. Just anything that might help us figure out who they are. Did they say where they came from, why they were there?"

"First they said they'd be working with Roy Granger at the Institute, then—Oh, no."

"What?"

"Roy. It's got to be Roy. We broke up recently, but before that, he kept asking me questions about Sable. He wanted me to convince her to come to the FIRM for testing."

"What!" Jonas jumped up and turned beet red. "Son of a bitch! Why didn't I hear about this before?"

"The firm?" Malcolm asked. "What is that?"

"The Foundation for Infertility and Reproductive Medicine." Jonas spat. "It's been in all the papers lately. This is the asshole doctor you were dating?"

"Jonas, I had no idea. If I had known about Sable, I would never have said a word about her or the twins."

"Janis," Malcolm said. "It's not your fault. They've probably had feelers out all over the country looking for others like themselves. To them we're just specimens," he spat. "I want to know why these two wolves let themselves get mixed up with a lowlife who wants to exploit them."

"Money," Jude exclaimed. "He's probably paying them a fortune to collect his specimens." He choked over the words.

"I remember a time when we weren't much better than them." Jonas' voice caught in his throat.

"That's in the past," Malcolm reminded them. "The important thing now is to find your mate and boys and bring them home."

Janis couldn't look Macolm in the eye. "So you think Wade and Noah are definitely connected to Roy?"

"I'd bet my life on it."

God, she wanted to hate them. She couldn't reconcile the men who'd been gentle caring lovers with the monsters who'd taken her family. If it really was them, she wanted payback. Wanted to make them suffer. "So what's our next move?"

"Your next move is to get out of Dodge with Karin and my son."

"No. These men got me mixed up in this, and I need to make it right."

Malcolm looked at Janis's brothers, and they shrugged.

"She knows them. It might be helpful," Jonas said.

"Okay then. We go to Philadelphia and start with this Roy character."

"Do you think he's still there?" Janis asked anxiously.

"Yes. If we're lucky, he has no idea we're on to him, and he thinks his identity and position at the FIRM are safe. Hopefully we'll have the element of surprise on our side." Malcolm looked over at Karin. "You and Junior are taking a little vacation. Where do you want to go?"

"With you."

He smiled at her. "I promise when this is over, I'll come join you, and we'll have a real vacation."

"Okay then, make it someplace warm."

"Good idea. You pack while I call the airport. We're all leaving tonight."

"We'll go back to the ranch and grab a few things. Our place is closer to the airport. You pick us up there." Jonas was already on his feet. "And Malcolm, thank you."

"You can thank me when we get them back." Malcolm bent down and rubbed Ralf's muzzle. "Wish I could take you with us. You hold down the fort, boy."

* * * *

After all that had happened, it felt strange to be back in the city. Janis had her apartment to herself while the men settled in upstairs. They were sleeping in Jonas's old apartment. She'd never rented it when he went back home to Black Wolf. The building wasn't at one hundred percent occupancy so she'd decided to keep it available for their use. It turned out to be a good call.

It was four a.m., and she doubted anyone would be going to sleep. She made coffee while she waited for them to come downstairs and talk strategy.

The coffee was done brewing just as she heard a light knock on the door. Janis checked the peephole and then let the men inside.

Jude sniffed. "Coffee. Good, I feel like hell. Maybe it'll help."

But Janis's eyes were on Malcolm. His nostrils flared, and he walked toward the bedroom. She followed and stood by the door, watching him anxiously.

Malcolm sat on the bed, picked up a pillow and rubbed his nose over it. Janis clutched her stomach. Her guts rearranged themselves in her belly, and she thought she might be sick.

"It's them. The two I tracked in the woods." He shook his head in disbelief. "Where did they come from? And why are they kidnapping their own kind?"

"I think I have a plan," Janis said softly.

Malcolm looked up at her. "I'm all ears.

Chapter Eleven

The redhead looked surprised. Good. Roy would be too. The whole idea was to keep them off balance. It would have been even better to wait a few days rather than walk in on the heels of the abduction, but understandably, no one wanted to wait. "Is Dr. Granger in?" Janis asked sweetly.

"Let me check," the woman replied, just as sweetly. She got up and was already opening the door to Roy's inner sanctum. Didn't the bitch know how to use an intercom?

Janis tapped her foot and scanned the room while she waited. At last the door opened, and the redhead appeared.

"He'll see you now." She held the door open for Janis.

Janis ignored her and kept her eyes on Roy as she walked into his office. Seeing him sitting behind the desk brought back images of what he'd been doing the last time she stood in this room. She shook them off. He might be human, but he was more a wolf than the Lycans. She wanted to strangle him, but not because of the redhead. That was the least of what he'd done to her.

"Hello, Roy."

"Janis, how are you?" Roy stood and came around the desk. Inwardly, Janis smiled. Was he trying to prove he was keeping it in his pants?

"Oh, I'm okay." She tried to put a wistful tone in her voice.

Roy took her hand, and she fought to keep herself from snatching it back. "Believe it or not, I'm glad to see you, Janis," he told her. "I feel badly about the way we ended things. I owe you an apology"

"I understand how things can get ugly in the heat of the moment, and I accept your apology. It's all water over the dam now."

"I'm glad you feel that way. Have a seat." He gestured to a chair and took a seat next to her. "Can I get you something? A drink?"

"No. Thank you." Janis crossed her legs and composed herself. "I need advice. Expert advice. You're the only person I felt I could turn to."

"I'm always here for you. I hope you know that."

Janis smiled. If the bastard was really involved, he'd be fishing for information pretty soon. "I do know that, Roy. Just like I know you're the best in your field."

He smiled slyly. "Are you trying to get pregnant? Or is this about your unusual family?"

"Neither." Janis frowned. "I don't hear from my family as much as I'd like. They seem to have forgotten about me since I moved here." She hesitated, wanting his curiosity to grow.

"That's too bad. Our families don't always behave the way we want them to." Roy sat back and waited for her to continue.

"This concerns a friend. A friend of my sister-in-law's actually. She lives out of state. I only met her once when she flew in to see the twins." Was Roy that good at keeping his composure or did this really mean nothing to him? She wanted him to be involved because he would be a solid link to Sable and the boys. On the other hand, she hated to think she'd been used by a master manipulator.

"Go on," Roy said.

"She's pregnant, and she wants to terminate it. She called me because she knew my sister-in-law would try to talk her out of it. And she thought I was still dating a doctor."

"Philadelphia is a big city with a lot of doctors and clinics. Why come to me?" Roy asked.

"This is the strange part. She's very secretive. Wouldn't tell me who the father is or where she's staying. I think the man has been abusing her. She might even be on the run."

"That's unfortunate. I might be able to help her, but I have to know where she is."

"I don't have a phone number for her, but she's calling me back tonight at ten in the evening."

"How about if I stop by? I can talk to her. Reassure her. Best case scenario, I can convince her that I'll keep her situation in the strictest confidence if she comes to see me."

Bingo!

"Roy, you don't know how relieved I am to hear you say that. I've been so worried about her, and I didn't know where to turn."

"I'm glad you came to me, Janis. I'll take good care of your friend."

* * * *

Before Janis saw Roy, Malcolm had her rub her dirty sheets all over her body. If Roy smelled a wolf, Malcolm didn't want it to be his scent. Janis thought it worked. Roy hadn't seemed suspicious in the least. Of course he was probably human and couldn't tell the difference between a Lycan and a stray dog.

When she got back to her building, she went to straight to Jonas's apartment so Malcolm could give her the sniff test.

"What do you think?" she asked him.

"He's a wolf," Malcolm said, disgust evident in his voice.

"I could have told you that," Janis said wryly.

"A real wolf, a Lycan."

Her jaw dropped, any attempt to lighten the mood forgotten.

"I was hoping he wasn't. I hate knowing my people are doing this to one of their own. Your brothers covered my scent in your apartment as best they could. I won't be going back in until it's time. Be careful around Roy," he cautioned. "He's a lot stronger than you, and if he shifts, he's lethal. Make sure you put the sedative in his wine. It's not enough to knock him cold. We want to be able to question him. But hopefully it'll slow him down."

Janis stomach did flip-flops. Now that she knew what Roy was, the thought of being alone with him terrified her.

"You're not getting cold feet, are you?" Jude asked.

"No. I can do this. I want to do this."

"Good girl." Jonas came over and gave her a hug. "Remember the code words. When your phone rings, if you're not ready say, *call me right back*. If it's a go, just say *I have someone here who can help you*. Remember you'll only be alone with him for a short time. Got it?"

"Yes." She hoped she didn't pass out when the phone rang.

Chapter Twelve

Janis's small apartment smelled like sex. Evidently her brothers had rubbed those well-used sheets on every surface. Janis knew it had been necessary to cover Malcolm's scent, but the aroma reminded her more than ever of what was missing in her life.

The initial disgust that she felt when she realized she'd bedded wolves had dissolved. A disconcerting mix of hatred and lust remained. She wanted revenge for the hurt these monsters had caused her family, but the intoxicating scent of Wade and Noah kindled a heat in her belly that threatened to become permanent.

As soon as all this was over, she intended to fumigate the apartment, rent it out, and move into another. Then she would throw herself into her studies and forget about men—and wolves.

Speaking of which, Roy would be here any second. Wine chilling—check, ketamine in the drawer—check, cell phone charged—check. Nothing more to do besides wait.

At exactly nine forty-five, a light knock brought her up short, and her blood ran cold. Roy was always punctual. She checked the peephole first, then opened the door.

Roy smiled and handed her a beautiful bouquet of yellow roses and baby's breath. At least the bastard hadn't brought red roses. She might have thrown them at him.

"Thank you, Roy. They're lovely." Janis took the flowers and buried her nose in them while she composed herself. "Come in."

Roy stood in the center of the room. Did his nostrils flare or did she imagine it?

"You look lovely, Janis."

"Thanks." She'd worn a tight blue dress that matched her eyes and a pair of fuck-me heels. Let the creep think she wanted to seduce him. "Have a seat."

"So how have you been?"

Like he really cared. "Busy. Classes start up soon, and I've been thinking about hiring more help to deal with the rentals."

"Good idea. I guess this business with your friend comes at a bad time."

He certainly didn't waste any time. "Yes, it's been rough." Janis sighed heavily. "How about some wine?" She would have missed his impatient frown if she hadn't been watching him so closely.

"Wine would be nice."

"Red?"

"You remembered." Roy smiled at her.

Janis wanted to spit at him. "Of course. It hasn't been that long." She couldn't wait to get in the kitchen and let out a deep breath. How had she ever let him touch her?

"Need some help in there?" Roy called out.

Shit! She better get a move on. "No, I'll be right in." Janis poured the Ketamine in a wine glass and filled it with merlot. Thank God, Jonas's degree came in handy for something. Being a doctor, he had no trouble obtaining the veterinary drug.

She poured herself a glass of white zinfandel and prayed she wouldn't spill the wine before she got back in the living room.

Roy accepted the glass and held it up to the light to admire the color. Her heart just about stopped. Did he suspect something?

"To old friends." He held the glass out, and she tapped it with hers before taking a healthy drink. The wine burned a warm path to her stomach and calmed her a bit.

"So tell me more about your friend."

"Well, as I said, I really don't know her all that well. I was shocked when she called me. We only met once, but I got the distinct impression that she had no family or friends to speak of."

"It does sound like abuse," Roy said. "A controlling man will separate a woman from her family."

Like you, you arrogant bastard.

Christ, she wished this was over. It was so damn hard to sit here and make nice when she wanted to kill him. She looked in his eyes, hoping to see a sign of fatigue.

"So what does this woman look like?" Roy took a big drink of his wine.

Janis raised her brows. "Why? Is that important?"

"Oh, I was just wondering if she had any bruises."

Yeah, right. "Not that I noticed." Good thing Jonas had told her that the Lycans healed quickly or she might have slipped and made up something about black and blue marks. "It did strike me as funny that she resembles my sister-in-law so much. Sable told me they're not related, but they look enough alike to be sisters."

Roy's eyes definitely lit up. He was in this up to his fangs.

"Perhaps there a familial connection way back in their past. At any rate, I hope I can be of some help."

The familiar tone of her cell startled Janis. *Showtime.* This was it. Had the drug affected Roy at all? She couldn't tell, but she didn't want to wait. Roy wasn't dumb, and if he thought she was stalling, he'd leave, or worse.

"Shouldn't you get that?" Roy yawned and covered his mouth. "Sorry. It's been a long day."

Thank God! Janis got up to retrieve her cell.

"Hello." Janis listened to Malcolm caution her to be careful. She looked at Roy. He placed his empty wine glass on the coffee table and rubbed his eyes with the heels of his hands. Inwardly, Janis smiled. Outwardly, she frowned. "I have someone here who can help you."

She closed her cell phone and rejoined Roy. "She's desperate. She wants to talk to you—in person."

Roy's face lit up. "How soon can she get here?"

The door flew open and slammed against the wall.

Janis couldn't help screaming at him, "She's here now, mother fucker!"

Roy jumped up with a lethal grace that didn't reveal an ounce of fatigue. His eyes darkened, and his lips curled back. He snarled viciously at Malcolm. "Who the fuck are you?"

Malcolm's laugh was truly frightening. "Someone you can't subdue so easily. Where's the woman and the children?"

Roy tore at his shirt. "Whoever you are, you won't live long enough to find out."

Malcolm, dressed in sweat pants only, had stripped bare before Roy had his clothes off. He crouched and leaped, shifting in midair and knocking Roy off his feet. Roy shifted. His buttons popped, and when his muzzle lengthened, he tore at his slacks with long yellow fangs.

Malcolm wrapped his limbs around Roy and snapped at him. Roy sang his fangs into Malcolm's leg and held on for dear life.

Janis's heart beat a staccato rhythm. She backed away in shock and fear. She knew Malcolm had no intention of killing Roy, only subduing him. But Roy was out for blood. Where the hell were her brothers?

Almost as if he'd read her mind, Jude ran through the door, Jonas behind him.

"Shit." Jude took aim with the tranquilizer gun. If he hit Malcolm, they were finished.

Malcolm wrenched the black wolf around until Jude had a clear shot at its back. He howled in pain as Roy's fangs tore at his limb.

Jude took a shot, and at last, the black wolf loosened its hold and lay still on the floor. Malcolm lay next to Roy, panting and licking at his wounded leg. In a few minutes, he sat back on his heels, a naked man looking at a wounded arm that had already stopped bleeding.

* * * *

Janis and Jude sat in her living room. The black wolf, tightly secured with chains, slept off the drugs in Janis bedroom.

Malcolm was fairly certain that the wolf would stay a wolf rather than talk. Roy knew they wouldn't kill him. He was their only link to Sable and the twins. It had been a calculated risk. They had no choice but to take it. That was the bad news.

On the other hand, they now had Roy's car and his keys in their possession. Malcolm and Jonas had already left to search Roy's office. With Roy's BMW parked in the garage, any activity noticed by security would hopefully be attributed to Roy.

Janis stretched out on the couch and watched Jude pace. She knew he didn't like being left behind.

"Malcolm only took Jonas because he's a doctor and might catch something important."

"I know. I just want to be doing something."

"You already have. If it wasn't for your shot, Roy might have gotten away, and they wouldn't have his keys."

"I'm going to take a look at our prisoner. Maybe we'll get lucky and he'll change back."

Janis sighed. She wanted to be doing something too. She wouldn't say it to Jude, but she felt every minute that passed since his family went missing put them further away from finding them. She stretched out on the couch and tried to think of any details she might have forgotten. Her eyes got heavy, and she closed them for just a few minutes.

Janis woke to growls and scratching noises coming from the bedroom. The first light of dawn showed through the blinds, and she smelled fresh coffee. Jude came out of the kitchen and handed her a mug.

"Here, take mine. I'll pour another cup."

"I can't believe I fell asleep." Janis took the coffee gratefully. "Any word?"

Jude shook his head. "No, but our houseguest is awake."

"I heard him." She took a sip. "I know they'll—"

The door opened, and she looked up, heart pounding. The men looked grim. That didn't bode well.

Jonas shut the door and locked it. Malcolm tilted his head toward the bedroom.

"Yeah, it's awake," Jude muttered. "Did you find anything?"

"Enough," Malcolm stated. "Thanks to Jonas." He nodded at her brother. "We have good reason to believe they're in New Mexico."

Janis's breath hitched. *New Mexico!*

"At first we came up empty. Then Jonas got on the computer. It took him hours to hack into Roy's emails, and we still didn't find anything useful."

Jonas picked up the story. "I looked through his sent folder. He had replied to an email, confirming a drop off location for a package. The Gila Forest in New Mexico. Good thing we got longitude and latitude. It's over three million acres of terrain that ranges from deep canyons to rugged mountain."

"How soon do we take off?" Jude asked breathlessly.

"Later this afternoon," Jonas said. "I already booked a flight on the way back here."

"What about our pet?" Jude asked.

"He'll have to ride in the cargo section with the other dogs." Malcolm grinned.

Chapter Thirteen

It had been a long time since Alex had a man in his bed, seven months to be exact, Roy's last visit home. He stroked his flaccid dick, hoping the sight of Sable lying naked and spread-eagled on the bed would entice him. It didn't.

Not even the thought of having his own child again aroused him. He wasn't even sure he wanted another child. When he'd lost his son, he swore he'd never father another. It hurt too much to lose them.

For a long time, he'd been content to be the unofficial elder and have Noah by his side. They didn't need children, because they had each other.

He'd loved Noah, still did if he let himself admit it. But he could never bring himself to tell him. Falling in love only led to heartache. Besides it seemed disloyal to his mate's memory. When Noah looked elsewhere for the affection he couldn't give him, Alex's jealousy, unreasonable though it was, overwhelmed him.

Noah wanted him to include Wade in their relationship, but the green-eyed monster inside Alex wouldn't allow it. When Roy made overtures to him, he took the man to his bed. He didn't have the same feelings for Roy, but a malicious part of him wanted to make Noah jealous. He hoped Noah would give up Wade and come back to him. Instead Noah drew further away, and the rift between them grew too wide to cross.

Roy had been studying in Boston when they found him and his head was filled with plans to help their people increase their dwindling numbers. Careful investing over the years had made their clan rich, but what good was it if their people were dying off? It was

Alex's idea to send Roy to Philadelphia for his fellowship and the clan's money had funded the addition to the hospital. Roy wanted Alex to come with him, but that was impossible. Their people needed him here. Roy hadn't been happy to leave him, but he had no choice. After all, it was his prodding in the first place that started all this.

Alex didn't want his race to die out. Now he wondered if it was all worth it. He wasn't happy. His people weren't happy. They'd been reduced to breeding with strangers instead of mates.

Sable turned her head. Good. He didn't want to see the tears in her eyes. In the back of his mind, he'd believed that once she was surrounded by her own kind she would realize that this is where she belonged. He knew now that would never happen. She already had a family she loved. He left the room, slamming the door behind him.

Alex saw Ayala, stationed outside the room where the half-breeds slept. She bowed her head as he passed. Little high-pitched cries and howls stopped him in his tracks. He turned on his heel, walked back and entered the room.

Empty save for a dresser and a crib, the adobe walls painted white. The tiled floor offered the only color in the room.

Taken aback, Alex looked down at the babies, clad in diapers and nothing else. *They almost sound like pups. But with that blonde hair and those blue eyes they look nothing like Lycan whelps. Doesn't the mother realize that she's brought demon half-breeds into the world?* Eventually they would let their human side take over and they'd turn into conquering bullies. Why should they live when his son had been murdered?

You're no better than the monsters that killed your family.

He tried to shut out the thought, but it wouldn't go away. Revisiting the painful void where he'd locked the memories of his wife and child almost brought him to his knees. Could he inflict the same hurt on someone else? Separate a mother from her children? What would his mate think of him if she saw him now?

"Ayala!" he screamed.

The girl came running into the room. She stood by the crib, shaking, head down.

"Take them to their mother before I change my mind."

"Yes, Alpha." The girl struggled to lift the squirming boys. Alex narrowed his eyes at her, and she got a firmer grip on them and made a hasty exit.

* * * *

Alex lay on his bed, thinking and staring into the dark. This wasn't the outcome he'd planned for, but it was the one that would allow him to sleep at night.

Noah and Wade were loyal, but they were filled with guilt over what they'd done. What he made them do. He didn't want to wait until morning to ease their minds.

Like a man possessed, he threw on a pair of trousers and padded out into the hallway.

Noah opened the door to his knock. Over his shoulder he saw Wade in their bed. Red-hot anger and jealousy almost made him turn away but Noah was right there, pulling him into the room.

"What's wrong?" Noah turned a light on and Wade sat up, a worried look on his face. "The babies?"

Gods. What had he turned into? His men actually thought he would hurt innocent babies. "They're with their mother."

"Then she's agreed to do what you want?"

"No. I changed my mind. I don't want her here."

"I don't understand. What are you going to do?"

"I'm sending her home, Noah. You and Wade take her and her spawn back to Pennsylvania tomorrow. Make sure she realizes it would endanger her family, as well as ours, if she reveals our location."

Noah grabbed him and pulled him close. "Thank you." He planted a chaste kiss on his lips.

Alex pulled back. "Noah, I—"

Loud voices and banging at the door stopped him from telling Noah how much he regretted what he'd done. The look on Noah's face told him that he already knew.

* * * *

Janis had a bad feeling that it had all gone terribly wrong. The rescue party had rented a cheap motel room near the airport. Malcolm, filled with bitter bloodlust, had headed straight for the coordinates while they stayed behind. Only he, with his Lycan scent could get inside without being immediately detected. He'd promised not to take any foolish risks, just try to find out where the captives were being held and then call to tell them how to proceed. Only it was taking way too long.

Finally Jude voiced what she had been thinking. "It's been hours. I don't want to wait any longer.

Janis went ballistic when her brothers told her to stay in the motel with an unconscious Roy. She felt responsible for putting her family in danger and she threatened to follow on her own if they didn't take her. They finally agreed. Each one wore something of Roy's, hoping it would disguise their scent. Janis took the gun Jude offered, hoping she wouldn't need to use it.

They parked a good distance from the site and walked, hoping their black clothing would offer some camouflage in the darkness. Janis thought she'd stepped back in time when the adobe pueblos appeared in her view. As they got closer, the multi-story housing structure reminded her of an apartment complex with connecting units.

Jonas had them stop to reassess their plan. What plan? Her brothers were acting for her sake. She knew they were winging it. What could they do against an army of men who could turn into wolves?

Janis swallowed her fear. There was no place for it here. They needed to keep their wits about them. The stakes were too high.

From where they hid behind a boulder, they could make out a lone figure standing guard. Jonas suggested taking him hostage. He crept off to scout the surrounding area and check for other watchdogs.

Janis kept her eyes on the guard. Another man came outside and spoke to him then they both looked toward the boulder. It was time to move on. Where was Jonas? "Jude, let's go," she whispered. "Dammit. Answer me." She turned and saw her brother on his knees, a gun barrel pointed at his temple. "Jesus God!"

Jude looked up, and she knew the other guards were behind her. *We're going to die.* She could only hope Jonas had gotten away.

* * * *

The Lycans took their weapons and escorted them to the building at gunpoint. Janis and her brother were shoved into Sable's room. Jonas was already there, holding her. It was a tearful reunion. Her brother had examined Sable and the babies from head to toe. Satisfied there were no signs of abuse, they finally questioned her, hoping they could find a way out. Janis feared for Malcolm. Would they kill one of their own?

Loud footsteps coming towards Sable's room struck terror in Janis's heart. The door opened, and Malcolm bruised and bleeding, was roughly shoved into the room at gunpoint. Four very large Lycans stood scowling at him. He must have put up a hell of a fight.

"Everybody get comfortable." The larger of the men gestured with his gun. "Have a seat."

Janis sat trembling on the bed. Sable sat on the floor with Jude and Jonas while Malcolm remained standing.

"What do you intend to do with us?" Jude asked.

"That's up to the Alpha," he sneered. "But we don't have much use for humans here."

Sable snarled at him. She looked like she might leap on him and try to tear him apart, but Jonas held her back.

Janis shut her eyes and directed a silent prayer heavenward. When she opened them, a tall, dark man in black leather pants blocked the doorway. When he stepped inside, Noah and Wade followed.

Oh God! A pulse thrummed deep in her womb, an aching desire to be filled. She stared at them, surprised at the sudden heat their appearance kindled in her. Tamping down her arousal, she hardened her heart. Flights of sexual fantasy were indulgences she couldn't afford, not when her family was at the mercy of these animals.

"Janis," Wade said, and started toward her, but one glance from the taller man stopped him in his tracks. Noah stared at her, his expression flat.

The tall man scrutinized her, and she glared back, determined not to cower in front of him.

The men with the guns acknowledged their leader by nodding, but they kept their weapons trained on Malcolm and her family.

The Alpha turned his attention to Malcolm. "Hello, brother."

Malcolm showed his teeth. "I have no brothers."

"And here I thought you came to join my pack."

"I came to rescue my family."

"Then the she-wolf is yours?"

"Sable is the sister of my dead first-mate."

The Alpha smiled grimly at him. "And who is the second-mate?"

Malcolm kept his silence.

"This one?" The Alpha tilted his head toward Janis. "So you can make blond-haired sons, too?"

Malcolm said nothing.

Janis snuck a look at Noah. He was glaring at Malcolm, and one corner of his mouth curled, revealing his teeth. Wade did the same.

The Alpha looked from one to the other. He took it all in and approached Janis. He sniffed the air around her and lifted her chin with his forefinger. "I think not. She's already been claimed, and by more than one wolf. Maybe I'll let them keep her for a pet."

"You son of—" Jude started to rise, but one of the men put a gun to his head. Sable cried out and pulled him back.

Janis snuck a look at Noah. She needed to know what would happen to them. Maybe she could talk to him on a personal level. If only she was better at reading people. His expression didn't reveal much, but she had to try. "Are you going to kill us?"

Noah looked shattered. He took a step toward her. "Janis, I would never hurt you. Please believe me."

"If you care anything for me, please don't hurt my family." Her voice broke and her eyes misted.

Wade came closer. He put a hand out to touch her, but she pulled back. The hurt in his eyes just about killed her. "I promise no one will be harmed." The words were for her, but he looked daggers at the Alpha.

Common sense dictated that she question whatever they said. She'd be a fool to believe any of them. And yet all her instincts told her she could trust Noah and Wade.

Malcolm snarled and approached them."Let's make a deal,"

"And what can you offer me?" The Alpha turned to Malcolm, grinning. He seemed to be enjoying this.

"Your doctor. I'll trade him for my family."

"Your she-wolf is more valuable to me. She can give me many pups. Between us, we can rebuild our dying race."

"If you touched her, I'll kill you." Jonas struggled to rise. Sable held him back and grabbed Jude when he made a move.

"No one touched me," she cried. "I swear it."

The Alpha watched them impassively. Malcolm's low growl brought the Alpha's attention back to him. "She already has a family. You have no right to her. The old laws would have you punished."

"Thanks to the humans, there are no old laws, nor elders to enforce them. We make our own laws here." The Alpha eyed Janis up and down like a piece of meat. "Here's my deal. Leave the blonde woman and the rest of you can go."

"No." Sable jumped up. "Let them all go, and I'll stay willingly."

"The hell you will," Jonas yelled. "Nobody is staying." He and Jude jumped up and flanked Sable.

The Alpha turned to Noah and Wade. "The disposition of the blonde female is entirely up to you."

Janis looked from one to the other. The men seemed too shocked to answer.

"Think about it." The Alpha turned to his guards. "Keep them here. We'll make arrangements for them to leave tomorrow when we get our doctor back. I'll find another room for this one." He nodded at Janis. "Wade, Noah, come with me."

"Alpha." Noah stood his ground. "You said—"

"I said come with me." His face darkened. "We need to talk."

Chapter Fourteen

Janis held Sam while Sable nursed Max. Hot tears welled up. She might never see her nephews again. Or her brothers.

A knock at the door startled both of them. Janis hugged Sam tight to her chest and opened the door. The young woman called Ayala stood there.

"Will you come with me please?"

Sable and the men started to argue, but Janis broke in. "It's okay. I'll see you in the morning." *I hope.*

Janis followed Ayala out the door and watched her lock it. "How can you live with yourself?" she asked Ayala. The woman remained silent and led her down a complex system of interconnecting hallways. They all looked the same with their white walls and tiled floors.

Janis tried to get her bearings, but she felt like a rat in a maze. They descended a few steps, then an incline, more steps. They were taking her to a dungeon, keeping her separated from her family. She wouldn't even have the comfort of a last night with them.

Janis grabbed Ayala's arm. "Where are we going?"

"To the baths. So you can clean up before bed."

"I don't want to clean up. Just take me to my room," Janis insisted.

Ayala wouldn't look at her. "I was told to bring you here."

"Told by who?"

Ayala shook her head and kept walking.

It had to be the Alpha. What did he have in store for her? Whatever it was, she deserved it. How could she have been so stupid to get mixed up with Roy?

They finally stopped before a heavy wooden door. Ayala opened it, and Janis stepped cautiously inside. The cavernous room, dimly lit by sconces on the painted adobe walls was like no bathroom she'd ever seen. In the shadowy center, steam rose from the bubbling water of a rectangular pool.

The setting, although calm and serene, frightened her.

"Ayala?" The girl was already gone. Janis ran to the door, not surprised to find it locked. Did they mean to keep her here? She turned and looked around her prison. From the corner of her eye, she spotted movement along the far wall. Her breath caught in her throat, and she backed up against the door.

It was only shadows, she told herself. She didn't see anything else. Janis let out a breath and took a few steps toward the pool, a hot spring. A stack of thick towels and a white robe, neatly folded, were laid out on the side.

The water looked hot. Janis kicked off her sneaks and dipped her toes, surprised to find it pleasantly lukewarm. A bath might not be such a bad idea. Sighing, she shimmied out of her jeans and slipped off her shirt.

Two submerged steps ran around the perimeter of the bath. She stepped down and sat at the edge with her feet in the water. The mosaic tiles at the bottom caught her attention. She leaned forward and tried to make out the design. The mist tickled her nostrils, and the earthy smell of sulfur made her lightheaded.

She felt so far removed from the city, like she'd been transported to another planet. Would this be her life from now on? Living among animals? Trying to coexist with the monsters that destroyed her family?

Were they all fiends? She suspected Roy and the Alpha were the perpetrators. She wanted to believe they'd coerced Noah and Wade into going along with their plan. But what difference did it make? They hadn't tried to stop it, so they were just as guilty as the others.

She had no choice but to comply. If she didn't, the Alpha might chain her up or worse. Didn't he say he would give her to the men as a pet? He hated her and everything about her, especially her blonde hair. Oh God. She might very well end up on a leash.

Somehow the thought of wearing a collar and sitting at Noah's feet didn't bother her as much as it should have. Seeing him and Wade put all those erotic fantasies back in her head. And even worse, they had stirred up all kinds of emotions and feelings she didn't want to revisit.

Damn them. Her men were too sexy for their own good. No, no, no. They were not her men. It was more like she belonged to them. Suddenly her body felt hot and heavy, her breasts achy. Her body betrayed her. How could she think of sex when she was being kept prisoner? Her fantasies were becoming her reality.

She pinched her nipples—hard—to wake her from this dreamy lethargy she found herself in. It didn't help. In fact she liked it way too much.

Her vulva, soft and swollen, seeped, and her own fluid wet her thighs. Janis slid a finger into the hot, wet slit of her sex. Her pussy lips parted, and her little bud stood erect and wanting attention. She circled it with her thumb, again and again. She leaned back, supporting herself with one hand, while the other tried to assuage the ache between her legs.

Lost in the pleasure, she imagined Noah's fingers in her cunt, Wade's hands on her breasts. A whimper escaped her throat, and she shut her eyes, teetering on the brink of release. She was so, so incredibly wet, and her thumb finally made contact with her clit and the spasms of orgasm made her shudder.

She opened her eyes and screamed.

The wolf sprawled by the edge of the pool and watched her intently. It pinned her with its golden stare.

Fear made the breath hitch in her throat, but the eyes held her enthralled. They were slightly slanted and closer together than a dog's, and they shone with human intelligence. Her fear melted. They were still Noah's eyes.

After a moment he nodded his massive head and laid it on top of his paws. What did it all mean? Why didn't he shift and do whatever he intended to do to her? The man kept his thoughts to himself, no matter what form he took.

"What do you want from me?"

He crawled closer. She moved back. He whimpered and stretched his head so his nose barely grazed her thigh.

Her gut told her he wanted to be touched. Janis had never touched a wolf before. *If I play along, maybe he'll help me escape.* Her hand hovered over Noah for a long moment before she lowered it. She patted his head for a brief second then jerked her hand away.

Noah whined and buried his head in her lap.

Janis gasped. He could nuzzle and sniff her sex all he wanted, but she wouldn't let him take her again without a fight. No. He and Wade would have to tie her down before she let that happen. More fluid leaked between her legs, and Noah growled. Not a scary growl, but the growl of a wolf who wanted to mate. She had no idea how she knew that, but she did. The hair on the back of her neck prickled.

"I don't know what you think is going to happen here," she told him, "but forget it."

He looked up her with soulful eyes that begged for acceptance. Could she? Her brothers loved Sable unconditionally and fathered children with her. Janis didn't feel any differently toward her. Of course she'd never seen Sable change into a wolf. That made it less real.

Janis slid her hand along Noah's back. She'd thought his fur would be like dog fur, but it was different. Up close, the rich color and lush texture of his coat was stunning, like Joseph's coat of many colors.

She stroked Noah's fur, loving the feel of it under her fingers. A contented rumble sounded in his chest.

"He's beautiful. Isn't he?"

Startled, she looked up at Wade. Her eyes went wide, like a kid caught with her hand in the cookie jar. She jerked her hand away from Noah's back and used it to cover her breasts. "Yes, he is."

"You don't have to stop." Wade crouched down next to her. Their nudity made her uncomfortable. It was different with Noah. It didn't embarrass her when he looked at her through wolf's eyes.

Wade was comfortable in his skin. Understandable with a body like his, but she didn't share the same comfort level with her body. She wondered if living here meant going without clothes most of the time.

Wade pulled her hands away and held them. "So are you, Janis. So beautiful." He released her hands and sat.

Janis turned away, not sure she believed him. "When I look at him like this it's hard to imagine him as Noah," she said softly.

"But he's still Noah. He sees you, feels you, understands what you say to him."

"Why doesn't he change?"

"He wants you to get used to him, like this."

Her heart sank. "Then you intend to keep me here."

She heard a noise like cracking twigs and turned. The fur receded, and Noah's human body emerged in a blur of shifting limbs and backbone. He sat back on his heels, stretched his neck, rolled his shoulders and flexed his fingers. "Do you like this better?"

She frowned at him. "I like when I can talk to you."

"You'll learn to understand me in both my bodies."

She shook her head. "Never."

Noah sighed. "Janis, I want you to know where we came from. Why we act as we do. My people were slaughtered by humans. We lost our families, our homes, everything. Your people were always the enemy."

"Why didn't you tell me this before?" Would it have changed anything? Probably not, but at least she would have known they confided in her.

"I couldn't. We pledged our loyalty to our Alpha. We owe him everything. He's the one who kept us alive after the massacre and led us to safety and our new home."

"And now he leads you to kidnap women and children," Janis spat.

"He wanted to increase our numbers." Noah looked away. "We were all afraid our race would die out. We'd been told we couldn't breed with human females, and of course, we couldn't reveal ourselves to the enemy. It was Roy's idea to concentrate on finding others like us and study ways to improve our fertility. And when Roy discovered the she-wolf, he convinced the Alpha that she belonged here with her own kind. But deep down our leader is a good man. His wife and baby were taken from him. He couldn't do the same to someone else. He planned to send her home before you and your men even got here."

Janis stared at him. "Is this true?"

Wade answered for him. "Yes, I heard the Alpha say it myself."

"Then why is he keeping me here?"

"He's not." Noah smiled wistfully. "We're not."

"But the deal?"

"There is no deal," Wade said. "You're free to leave with your family tomorrow. I've already told them we wouldn't force you to stay. Our Alpha liked your feisty ways. He thought you were very brave to come here and fight for your family. He thinks we made a wise choice and wanted to give us some time alone with you."

"Choice?" Janis's brow furrowed.

"There really was no choice," Noah said. "Not for you. Not for us. It's destiny. We marked you as ours." He traced a finger over the scar of his bite mark, then Wade's. "The Alpha thought we should have a chance to convince you to stay."

"Stay?" Janis couldn't wrap her head around it all, but one thing echoed in her head. She was free to leave. She wouldn't have to give up her family or her home. "I can leave? Tomorrow? For real?"

Noah frowned. "If that's what you want."

Janis threw her arms around him. "Oh, I do."

Noah held her tightly and looked into her eyes. "So be it."

She heard Wade slip into the water. Noah released her. He slipped his hand under the towels and retrieved a bar of soap and a sponge. He tossed the soap to Wade before he entered the bath. They both looked up at her. Their eyes glittered with hunger.

Janis's heart hammered against her chest. She felt herself slipping under their spell again, and she didn't want to fight it. Her body so attuned to theirs, it seemed as if they were already connected on some level. It was at once exciting and alarming.

"You're not our captive," Wade said softly. "You have nothing to be afraid of. Let us bathe you tonight."

The deep rumble of his voice made her cream flow. Of course they wanted more than a bath. So did she. Why shouldn't she enjoy them one more time? She would never find men like these back home. They were the stuff of a woman's wildest fantasy. A dream to lull her to sleep on lonely nights. She stepped into the water. Noah held out his hand, and she placed her palm in his.

* * * *

Noah stood in the bath and waited to see what Janis would do. When she took his hand, his heart fluttered wildly, and he took a deep breath to try and still it. At least she would leave them with this memory.

He'd never seen such an erotic sight in his life. Her skin was flushed, and her dilated pupils made her eyes darker. Currents of sexual desire seemed to float on the water between them.

They were connected on some deep level, as if she'd been created just for him and Wade. When she left there would be a void in their lives that no one else could fill. She wasn't immune to the magnetic link between them. She'd responded to it the first time they met in her office. Their bond couldn't be denied.

He studied her, wanting to preserve her beauty in his mind forever. He didn't blame her for wanting to leave. Not after what he and his people had put her through. After tomorrow, he wouldn't see her again. He had no illusions that she would come back and visit.

The water only reached to his thighs, and the evidence of his excitement was plainly visible. Her dark blue gaze slid down his body and fixed on his rampant erection.

His eyes fixed below her belly where the water licked at the gold curls between her thighs. He ached to bury himself inside that dark wet depth.

She looked like a beautiful statue as she stood there waiting. He walked behind her. She shivered when he ran a hand down her back.

Wade lathered his hands and passed the soap to Noah. Noah had chosen lavender. He'd smelled it in her bathroom in the city.

Together they washed her. Noah tossed aside the sponge and used his hands as Wade did. He caressed her ass then spread the oily soap between her cheeks. She tensed, and he whispered in her ear. "I'll never hurt you, Janis. Let me love you."

Wade lathered her breasts. Her dark nipples peeked through the bubbles, deliciously tempting. Wade had better access, and he spent a long time rinsing off the soap and then taking each hard tip in his mouth. He suckled one and then the other.

Wade released her breast with a soft pop. He lifted his head and kissed her. "You're so beautiful," he whispered against her mouth. "I've never wanted a woman like this before."

Noah knew it was true. He'd never heard anything remotely like that come out of his lover's mouth. The words didn't make him jealous. They only aroused him more, because he felt the same.

Noah watched motionless, unwilling to disturb their embrace, even though he wanted to take her to the ledge and fuck her senseless.

Neither of them had ever connected on such an intimate physical and emotional level with a female. Primal instinct had driven them to mark her, the sign of a true mate, as Alex had explained. Only Alex knew what it felt like to be truly mated. The others, including himself and Wade, had been young and single when they were driven from their home.

They'd never expected this—and certainly not with a human woman. If only she felt the same. Janis belonged to them, and they loved her, but their ways meant nothing to her. They couldn't expect her to love them back.

Noah couldn't stop touching her skin. The thrill of having her in his arms even exceeded the pleasure he'd once felt in Alex's arms. He knew that he and Wade could never have a real bond with Alex. It would undermine his role as Alpha, especially now that he and Wade had marked a human female. It was enough to know that Alex would always be there for him.

It didn't surprise him that Alex had grudgingly accepted these humans and made a tentative peace with them. The real Alex had been lost for a time, but he was back now.

This new compassion would be very welcome in the coming days. Already Noah missed his mate, and she was still here with him. No doubt he'd find comfort with Wade and Alex when Janis left them for good. But there would always be a part of him missing.

When at last Wade and Janis broke apart, Noah slid an arm around her waist and pulled her tight against him. His cock throbbed against her ass. The slippery feel of her body made him lose all rational thought, and a primal growl escaped his chest.

She reached up and back to clasp her hands behind his neck. Noah nuzzled her ear and flattened his palm over her mons. He swore he could hear her heart beat in her chest, until her moans and whimpers drowned it out. Wade fisted his cock and stroked it while he watched.

Noah nipped her ear and whispered to her, "Do you want more, Janis?"

"Yes. God yes," she hissed.

It pleased him that she still wanted them after seeing him in his wolf form.

Wade grasped her buttocks, and Noah her hips. She wrapped her legs around Wade's waist as Noah lowered her onto his lover's cock.

"Oh my God. You feel so good." Janis moaned and buried her face in Wade's neck. Slick from the oily lavender soap, Noah prepared to penetrate her from behind.

Janis shifted in Wade's arms to accommodate him, and Noah slid a finger inside her easily.

"More, Noah," she begged.

"Okay, baby. I just don't want to hurt you." He guided his cock to her tiny hole and entered her slowly.

"Yes," she hissed.

He pressed deeper, and she groaned at the double penetration. Noah stilled. "Are you okay?"

"Yes, Noah. Please don't stop."

He moved and felt Wade's cock through the thin layer of flesh separating them. It was heaven being connected like this. Janis wiggled and shifted between them. The scent of sex and arousal mixed with the sulfur, drugging him.

Noah slid one hand between Janis's body and Wade's to squeeze his lover's sac. Wade groaned, and Noah felt his fingers dig into his back. He caressed Wade's balls and then rubbed Janis's swollen clit while Wade thrust deeper inside her.

"Oh God, Noah." Janis trembled between them.

"I think our girl is liking this," Noah muttered. "Are you, Janis? Do you love having Wade's fat cock in your pussy and mine in your tight ass?"

Her answer was a guttural scream as his words brought on her climax. Her rhythmic contractions milked him, and he flooded her inside as he heard Wade's harsh groan of masculine satisfaction.

Chapter Fifteen

Janis woke in a bed, the dream fresh in her mind. Except it wasn't a dream. She really had been with Wade and Noah. Sandwiched between her two men, being thoroughly fucked, had to be the most erotic experience of her life.

The combination of their lovemaking and the relaxing heat of the hot springs had lulled them into a semi-comatose state. The men had spread the thick towels by the side of the pool, and the three lovers lay in each other's arms, totally comfortable with the intimacy. Janis, boneless and languid, had drifted off to sleep. She hardly remembered Noah carrying her here and laying her on the bed. No wonder she thought she'd been dreaming.

Envious thoughts filled her head. Her sister-in-law lived that fantasy every night. For a minute, she let her mind drift. She imagined a different life for herself. A life filled with love, and a family of her own. That was her real dream.

But that was Sable's life, not hers. What made her think she could satisfy two virile men? They weren't even real men. They were werewolves for God's sake.

But when she pictured them, it wasn't fur she saw, but Wade's sculpted face and thick black hair and Noah's amber eyes framed by long black lashes, always staring so seriously into hers. They always looked at her as if they expected something that she wasn't capable of giving them. She probably disappointed them sexually. She wasn't a she-wolf after all.

No wonder Sable had two husbands. One human man probably couldn't satisfy her. Good thing her brothers didn't seem to mind. They both loved her.

Love, the dreaded L-word. Look where it had gotten her. Her breath caught. Where did that come from?

Admit it, girl. You've already fallen head over heels.

She couldn't be in love with Wade and Noah. Look what they'd done to her family. Deep in her heart, she knew they were good men. They'd let their own hurt lead them astray, but they regretted it. She'd already forgiven them, and she didn't fear them. But they were so different.

Besides, they didn't have feelings for her. They were totally committed to each other. Today she'd leave New Mexico and in all likelihood never see them again. The thought was almost too painful to bear. She had to put it out of her head before it destroyed her.

Janis spied her clothes on a chair. She went into the small adjoining bathroom to dress. On the vanity she saw a stack of the same thick towels her men had used to dry her last night. She picked one up, hoping to catch their scent, but these were freshly laundered.

She really had to stop this. For sure they weren't trying to catch her scent. They would choose each other. Not her.

She stopped short. What had Noah said last night?

They had marked her as theirs, and the Alpha thought they'd made a wise choice.

At the time it went right over her head. She'd been so excited at the thought of going home she didn't hear anything else. What did it mean? Was their mark some kind of brand, like a rancher would put on livestock? Is that how they saw her? How dare they? Animals keeping humans for pets.

She didn't need a shower, but she took one anyway. She wanted to wash off any marks they'd left. The scars on her shoulders had faded. She couldn't wait until they disappeared.

Janis dressed in her jeans and sweatshirt and went to find her family. Her nephews' cries led her down the hall to their room. Jude opened the door to her knock and pulled her inside.

Malcolm stood in the corner. The babies were lying on the bed, fussing because they didn't want to get dressed.

"They want to be naked, like little pups." Sable laughed.

Janis looked at her horrified. Her nephews were not dogs.

Sable didn't notice her expression. She hugged Max and kept one hand on a squirming Sam.

"We're leaving, Janis," Jude stated. "All of us."

"I know." Janis hugged him.

Malcolm stepped forward, frowning. "I don't believe it." He shook his head. "It's a trap."

"No," Janis assured him. "Wade and Noah told me last night. Their Alpha planned to send Sable home before we even got here. And he never intended to keep me a prisoner."

"Then why the charade?" Jonas asked.

Janis looked away. "It's complicated."

A firm knock had them all looking toward the door. Malcolm strode over and opened it.

"I've come to take you to breakfast." Ayala stood there.

Thank God. Saved by the bell.

They followed Ayala to a large dining room where a long wooden table was set with vibrantly colored plates, each one with a different bird painted on it. Janis sat between Jonas and Malcolm.

She fiddled with the flatware. When she looked up, the wolves were entering the room. Noah caught her eye, and she turned away.

The Alpha sat across from her, Noah on one side, Wade on the other. Ayala and a young man made several trips from the kitchen with covered serving bowls and pots of fresh coffee.

Wade and Noah uncovered dishes of fluffy scrambled eggs, ham, blueberry corn pancakes, and tortillas. Janis's mouth watered.

For several awkward moments, they silently passed plates and tried to avoid eye contact.

The Alpha cleared his throat. "I want to apologize to all of you. I'm sorry for causing you distress." He looked at Sable. "I envy you for the happiness you've found with your mates, and I assure you that your family will not be bothered again."

"And the sister of my heart is free to go with us?"

Janis turned to Sable, touched by her words.

"Of course. If that's what she wants," the Alpha answered.

Everyone turned to look at Janis. *Is it?* The words stuck in her throat. She wrapped her arms around her waist and tried not to think about how right it felt to be in Wade and Noah's arms. They don't love you, she told herself.

"Is that what you want, Janis?" the Alpha asked her.

"I want to go with my family," she whispered.

"Are you satisfied?" Jude said harshly.

"Yes." The dark-haired man stared at her intently. "Of course she's free to leave."

The rest of the meal went by in a blur. She was dimly aware of some discussion about Roy. Evidently, he'd been brought back to the compound, none the worse for being drugged, and would return to Philadelphia to continue his research, Thank God, he hadn't joined them. She never wanted to see him again.

Why didn't she feel happier? Instead she felt like she was making the biggest mistake of her life. Suddenly, she couldn't eat another bite. Shortly after, she excused herself and left the room, and promptly got lost. When she found a door leading to a patio, she stepped out to catch her breath.

The door opened behind her, and she whirled around to see the Alpha standing there, leaning against the frame. She backed away.

"I'm not here to hurt you, Janis. I only want a few words with you in private," he told her. "When I apologized earlier, I meant it. I take full responsibility for what was done to you and your family. Please don't blame Wade or Noah. What they did, they did on my orders. I can see now how wrong I was, but Wade and Noah have strong loyalties to me and their people."

"I understand family loyalty," Janis said.

"I don't think you do."

Janis's back went rigid. "I'd do anything for my family."

"For your human family." He smiled at her. "I know you love them, just as I love my Lycan family. You don't want to see them hurt and missing you."

"Of course not," she said indignantly.

"Just like I don't want to see my family hurt and missing you."

"I don't understand," she said uneasily.

"I know, but you've been marked."

"Marked? You mean branded like an animal."

"I mean marked like a true mate. A wife."

Her heart fluttered in her chest.

"I had hoped Wade and Noah would make this clear to you last night."

Her face went hot.

"I guess you didn't do much talking." He sighed. "It's the way with mates. We're very physical. We show our emotions more than speak of them." He sighed. "And we've been hurt. Some of us, myself more than the others, have trouble expressing our feelings. It doesn't mean they don't run deep. Our bites are signs of love and commitment. If you leave, they'll be bereft. I suspect you will too. You're not Lycan, but I can see by the way you look at them that you love them. You belong together."

"I don't know what you're talking about. I don't belong here. I have a family and a life back in Philadelphia."

"You have a family here." He shook his head sadly. "If you'd only admit it to yourself."

He turned and walked back inside, leaving her staring after him.

* * * *

Jonas rapped on her door and poked his head in. "Are you ready?" She forced a smile. "Yes."

He picked up her bag, and she followed him out. Everyone was in the hall waiting for her. She saw Wade and Noah hanging back with the Alpha.

They usually hid their feelings well, but now, they looked wistful. Her heart twisted. She hated to see them unhappy. She wanted to run to them and throw herself in their arms.

Was it possible they really cared for her? Noah and Wade were in a committed relationship. Where did she fit in? Could they love her the way they loved each other or was she destined for heartache? She had to find out.

Janis approached her men and stood between them. Shaking in her shoes, she faced her family. She took Noah's hand in her right hand and Wade's in her left. She twined her fingers through theirs and held them to her heart. "I'm not leaving."

There was dead silence, except for the sharp exhales of breath from her men. She snuck a peek at the Alpha. He winked at her. Then she looked into Noah's eyes. She knew immediately that she was doing the right thing. He kissed her, and she turned to Wade, who smiled and kissed her back.

Then all hell broke loose. Her family crowded around her, demanding an explanation and looking daggers at the wolves. How could she explain that somehow she knew she belonged here?

She released her men and pulled aside the collar of her shirt. "I'm a marked woman." Surely they all knew what that meant. Or did only the men mark the women? She knew so little about Lycan culture. All she could do was follow her heart. She looked at Sable. "I can't leave my men. I won't leave them."

Sable walked toward her. "Of course you can't. No more than I can leave mine." She hugged her. "Believe me I understand. Your brothers and I went through some hard times until we realized we were meant to be together. Just give them some time. They'll come around."

She kissed everyone, and found it especially hard to let her nephews go. *Will I ever see them again?*

"You'll have one of your own soon," Sable assured her. "Don't believe what they tell you. Human and Lycan mates are perfectly capable of making babies together."

Janis laughed and looked at Wade and Noah. Did they even want children? They didn't look unhappy about the prospect.

The Alpha cleared his throat. "You'll see them again. Your family is always welcome here."

"And if you ever decide you want to come home, just call me. I'll come and get you." Jonas added.

"I'll be fine, but I will call you. A lot."

After more tearful goodbyes, Janis and her mates walked her family outside where the van was waiting. When they drove off, she suddenly felt shy.

Noah put his arms around her. He looked like he wanted to eat her up. "Want to check out your new bedroom?" He flashed a sinful grin.

"Lead the way."

They walked back inside and down a hall she hadn't seen before. Wade unlocked the door, and Noah swept her off her feet and carried her over the threshold. She laughed, and Noah frowned. "Isn't this how humans do it?" he asked.

"Yes, Noah. I was just thinking how very much I like the way wolves do it."

"So you like it doggy style, do you?"

"I like it anyway you'll give it to me," she purred.

"Did you hear that, Wade? Our girl wants us. Now."

He dropped her on the king-sized bed and followed her down. He started removing his clothes while she batted her eyes at Wade.

"Do you plan on double-teaming me?"

"You better believe it, sweetheart," Wade growled, throwing his own clothes to the far corners of the room. He pulled her sneaks off, and Noah started on her shirt. When she was bare, they both sat looking at her.

"What?" she asked.

"You're so beautiful," Noah told her.

"I could look at you all day," Wade said.

"I wouldn't mind getting touched a little."

Noah grinned and lay beside her, a hand on her breast. "Like this?" he murmured as he fondled and squeezed.

"Mmm. Yes. Just like that."

Wade's mouth found her other breast, and he sucked gently.

Noah moved his hand to her shoulder and rubbed his mark. "I'm glad you stayed. I would have gone after you if you hadn't, but it's so much better that you chose on your own."

She stared at him, too surprised to say anything.

"I love you. Did you think I'd give up on my mate so easily?"

"I didn't know I was your mate, Noah."

"And mine." Wade lifted his head. "I love you, too."

"So, you would have kidnapped me and dragged me back here like cavemen?"

"No," Noah said. "We would have moved back into our apartment and courted you until you saw the error of your ways."

"Well, maybe I will leave. I want some of that courting."

"Oh, we intend to court you," Wade growled. "Wolf style."

Her pussy clenched at the thought. "Oh, I love both of you so much." She kissed one, then the other.

Noah slid his hand over her belly and along her slick folds. "Gods, you're so fucking wet." His finger slid inside her, and she bucked.

"Court me," she begged.

A wicked smile creased Noah's face. "Time to eat, is it?" He slid down her body and moved between her legs. Nuzzling his face in the curls between her thighs, he brushed his nose over her clitoris, making her whimper. His fingers traced her labia, and he followed them with his tongue. "You taste so good. I can't get enough," he murmured. His long rough tongue lapped at her cunt before it slid inside her like a snake.

"So good." She looked into Wade's eyes. "Do you like watching Noah ravish me?"

"Can't you tell?" He took her hand and put it on his erection, and all her thoughts centered on the long, hard cock throbbing in her hand.

She was so aroused, so hot, wet, and aching for these two beautiful men to fuck her. "God, I want to eat, too, Wade."

He groaned and straddled her chest, and the tip of his cock nudged her lips. Janis swirled her tongue around the head and watched his eyes darken in response. He growled and thrust into her mouth. The rough hair on Wade's groin rubbed against her sensitive breasts and drove her crazy. She gripped his thighs and urged him deeper.

"I don't want to come yet," Wade grunted and pulled out of her mouth. Noah crawled up her body and rubbed his hard cock along the seam of her sex.

She grabbed his hair and arched up to meet him. "Oh God, Noah. Please. Fuck me!"

He slid his long length inside her, and a few strokes had him just where she wanted him, buried inside her pussy. She welcomed his invasion, wrapped her legs around his waist, and clung to him. His thrusts became harder, and her climax built. Suddenly she convulsed around him and sank her teeth in his neck. Noah howled and released his seed inside her.

He rolled, taking her with him, and she felt Wade at her back. Noah pulled her leg over his hip, and Wade rubbed something cool on her ass. He slid one, then two fingers inside her while Noah kissed her and rubbed her sensitive clit. Wade withdrew his fingers and positioned his cock against her ass. Excited, Janis pressed back against him.

"Gods, you feel so fucking good," he groaned as he slowly slid inside.

Both men started moving, fucking her relentlessly. She rocked between them, her need growing with each thrust. The feeling of being filled so completed enthralled her.

Wade reached around to play with her clit and leaned over her back to kiss Noah. Noah's strokes quickened, and Wade met them.

Warmth flooded her belly and spread through her body. As the spasms started, she twisted her head and bit Wade's neck under his jaw. He stiffened and growled. She was dimly aware of the men releasing their seed inside while her own climax took her body and soul.

They lay entwined for a few minutes, and then the men pulled away. Noah cupped her face. "I love you, baby." Then he leaned over her to kiss Wade. "And I love you."

"I love you," Wade told him, before kissing Janis and telling her he loved her.

Janis professed her love while she inspected her bite marks on their flesh. "And I think I just married you both."

"You did." Noah laughed.

Janis, deliriously happy, snuggled for a few minutes and enjoyed the close bond she felt with her men. Then she pinched them. "Hey, I still expect to be courted."

"Sweetheart, it's a promise," they both murmured in unison.

THE END

WWW.GALESTANLEY.NET

ABOUT THE AUTHOR

Gale always loved to read, especially fairy tales where marvelous things happened and a girl could grow up to be anything she wanted. She dreamed of being a writer and creating her own magical stories, but real life got in the way, and she put those dreams aside. When she heard the wakeup call, she took the plunge and escaped from cubicle hell. Now she has the best job in the world. She can be anything she wants and she doesn't mind living vicariously through the smokin' hot alphas and strong heroines she loves to write about.

For all titles by Gale Stanley, please visit
www.bookstrand.com/gale-stanley

Siren Publishing, Inc.
www.SirenPublishing.com

CPSIA information can be obtained
at www.ICGtesting.com
Printed in the USA
LVOW10s2339230717
542370LV00030B/1363/P